WENDY

On Kapiti Coast

Copyright © 2024 by Wendy M. Wilson

All rights reserved. No part of this publication may be reproduced, stored or transmitted in any form or by any means, electronic, mechanical, photocopying, recording, scanning, or otherwise without written permission from the publisher. It is illegal to copy this book, post it to a website, or distribute it by any other means without permission.

This novel is entirely a work of fiction. The names, characters and incidents portrayed in it are the work of the author's imagination. Any resemblance to actual persons, living or dead, events or localities is entirely coincidental.

Wendy M. Wilson asserts the moral right to be identified as the author of this work.

Wendy M. Wilson has no responsibility for the persistence or accuracy of URLs for external or third-party Internet Websites referred to in this publication and does not guarantee that any content on such Websites is, or will remain, accurate or appropriate.

First edition

This book was professionally typeset on Reedsy.
Find out more at reedsy.com

Contents

Dedication		iv
1	The Irishman	1
2	On the Road to Camp Russell	5
3	Bodies on the Beach	17
4	Palmerston North	29
5	Kate and Harry at the Royal Hotel	45
6	Kate Goes to Pahiatua	53
7	Harry in Pahiatua	65
8	Massey College	76
9	The Gunshot	87
10	On the Run	98
11	The Jeep	109
12	Uncle Joey	119
13	The Captive	128
14	Return to Massey College	133
15	The Internment Camp	144
16	The Pahiatua Police Station	152
17	The Chase	162
18	Back to Camp Russell	174
19	Pursuing the Traitors	184
20	The Man in the Jeep	195
21	Separation	205
22	Author's Note	213

Dedication

This book is dedicated to the ten U.S. Marines who drowned off the coast of New Zealand on June 20, 1943, during a training exercise.

Ten United States Navy personnel drowned off the Kāpiti Coast, north of Wellington, during a training exercise in bad weather. As wartime censorship prevented newspapers from publicizing the American presence in New Zealand, the incident was shrouded in mystery for decades. [1]

NOTE: As many as 45,000 U.S. Marines were in New Zealand in 1942 and 1943. They were training for the attack on Tarawa, a heavily fortified atoll. The attack on Tarawa began on November 20, 1943, and lasted three days. Casualties were heavy, but the Marines eventually prevailed.

---

[1] US Navy tragedy at Paekākāriki, URL: https://nzhistory.govt.nz/page/us-navy-tragedy-Paekākāriki, (Manatū Taonga — Ministry for Culture and Heritage), updated 28-May-2024

1

The Irishman

Kapiti Coast, June 20 1943

His trousers clung to his calves like wet seaweed, and the wind pushed him backward, whipping sand into his eyes and making it hard to move forward along the shell-covered beach. The tide was coming in and washing over his boots, and every step he took was an effort, his feet sinking into the muck as he forced out another step. He was completely knackered. Was he nearly there? He couldn't tell. For all he knew, he could be walking on the spot, using all his strength for nothing, while his footprints disappeared behind him.

When he'd delivered his message, he'd have to drag his arse the entire way back again and hope he could find his rowboat. *Make sure it's a good mile from the meeting place*, they'd said. *Those Marines from the camp they're all over the dunes with their weird amphibious vehicles or running along the beach carrying their heavy gear, night and day, they never stop. Don't want them to find a suspicious-looking boat or to see you lurking about.*

He asked himself, had it all been worth it, putting up his hand to volunteer to infiltrate a group of traitors? What was he going to get out of it? A firm handshake and the promise of a job as a constable? That he could have had back home without the threat of the draft hanging over his head in neutral Ireland. He'd been carried away by his kinship to the big man in this country, a very distant relationship at that. Their great-grandmothers were sisters or something like. Second cousins sixteen times removed? Who the fook knew? Just something the entire family always boasted about, and then someone said, 'Why don't you go there, Sean boy? Get ahead, you would.' And like an eejit, he came here. And then, like an even bigger eejit, he put his hand up when they asked for a volunteer.

The moon flickered briefly between the clouds, and he saw the pile of rocks outlined fifty yards away.

Thanks be to God, he was there at last. But no sign of his handler yet. Well, at least he could sit down, roll himself a smoke, look at the ocean, and admire the stars down here on the bottom of the globe. What a country. What a feckin' weird upside-down country.

He climbed halfway up the rocks and sat down. Bloody cold on his backside, but at least no sand whipping in his face up here, just wind. He pulled up his collar, rolled a smoke, and lit it up, making sure to shield the flare from the match in case someone had a bead on him. That was what they were told in the army, so he heard. No one had a bead on him here, of course, unless they were on a boat fifty yards out. Not likely in that surf. Enough to drown you in minutes, the towering waves and the currents and the undertow. Especially for someone like him who'd never learned to swim.

As if he'd conjured it up from his very own head, a boat appeared on the horizon. Not just a row boat like the one he'd left pulled up on the sand, but a massive warship. It was in the lea of the island out there, Kapiti Island, it was called. And smaller boats were spilling from it. Landing craft? He couldn't tell from here, but the ship hadn't hit an iceberg, so it wasn't lifeboats. Lots of them, though. Twenty, thirty. And all of them heading in his direction.

Wilhelm had better get a move on, or they'd be caught by the Yanks or whoever it was coming ashore. They had a camp up from this beach, the Yanks did. Of course, Wilhelm was a Yank, so he'd know what to say to them. From what he'd seen of him, he could talk himself out of anything. A very persuasive bloke, that Wilhelm. Knew what he wanted.

He heard the sound of someone behind him and craned his neck around. He could see the uniform but not the face. The moon had gone behind a cloud, and the person coming down the rocks was nothing more than a shadow. He put a hand in his pocket and clutched the list of names, the list he'd gathered for Wilhelm. And the reason why he was on this godforsaken beach at night.

"Yer here at last. Just in time, matey. Some of your pals are on the way in. See 'em?"

"Nothing to worry about," said a voice. A voice he didn't recognize.

"Wait, where's Wilhelm? I thought I was meeting Wilhelm?"

"Not this time."

He heard a click and started to rise to his feet. What the hell? A gun?

Wilhelm didn't carry a gun. He shoved his hand up to his mouth.

An explosion, and then darkness. No time even for a quick prayer.

Just time to shove the list of names deep into his throat.

2

On the Road to Camp Russell

Wellington, New Zealand: June 21st, 1943

Kate Hardy reluctantly opened the door to the news editor's office at *The Dominion*, hoping he didn't have another dull story for her to waste her time on. She was dying to have something exciting to write about — a fire at an insurance company, a train coming off the rails, even another battle between American and New Zealand soldiers like the one in Manners Street back in April when US soldiers had objected loudly to Māori soldiers entering the Allied Services Club.

Unfortunately, her editor had decided she was the best person to write women's stories about garden parties where scones were served smeared with jam made from turnips or stories about a group who'd knitted their way to 500 pairs of woolly socks for the troops, after first gathering clumps of wool from barbed wire fences and spinning it into yarn.

"Women are doing so much on the home front," he said. "We should celebrate them in the paper."

If she were a man, he'd be sending her out scanning the

waters for submarines from the deck of the Cook Strait Ferry or talking to injured soldiers returning from overseas about their battle experiences. Of course, if she was a man, she would have been called up to fight overseas months ago, so she shouldn't be complaining.

Her editor, Max Bauer, looked up, his eyes bright, smiling like a cat who had just caught a mouse and wanted her to play with it. Hope surged in her heart. Perhaps he did have something interesting for once.

"Kate, my dear. Have a seat. I've just had news that something strange is going on up on Kapiti Coast," he said as she pulled up a hard wooden chair. "At Camp Russell, the US Marine Corps training camp. The cooking staff were forbidden to enter this morning, and the milkman had to leave his bottles with the sentries at the gate to get warm. A chap I know telephoned me and said they're all down on the beach searching for something, and there are boats everywhere. He's watching them through binoculars, but he can't make out what's going on. All he can see is shadows moving around. You need to get up there and find out. Could be an enemy submarine skulking around. I've been waiting for another one of those since they sank the *Turakina* at the start of the war."

Kate Hardy sighed. War stuff. Weren't there any good disasters to cover?

"Why does it matter what the bloody US Marines are doing? Ask me to write about them when they leave. I'll enjoy that. I'll write a lovely description of them climbing the gangplanks of their troop carriers and sailing away forever."

He leaned towards her over his desk, his mustache quivering.

"Listen, Kate, I keep getting told by the War Office that I should shut up about the Marines training in New Zealand because the enemy will find out. But the bloody Prime Minister was in Washington last month and had a press conference to thank Americans for coming here to defend us. Even Tokyo Rose knows they're here. It's an open, bloody secret. So what's so important to them that has caused them to miss lunch and drink warm milk to stop it from getting out? It's got to be something big. I want to know what it is before the *Evening Post* gets hold of it."

"Can't you send someone else?"

"No, I can't. All I have are a few dozy old men and Mrs. Baker on the telephone. She won't budge, and the old men are useless. The war would be over before they got their bums off their seats."

He was right, of course. With all the men between twenty and fifty away fighting and demand for healthy older men at a premium, the newsroom was down to a half-dozen old men nodding off at their desks, a middle-aged woman permanently glued to the telephone, pencil in hand scribbling in a notebook, and a lad too young to enlist pulling updates off the wires. She was it as far as getting out there to investigate anything.

"I'm sick of war," she said. "I'm sick of New Zealand being overrun by gum-chewing Americans when our boys are dying thousands of miles away in North Africa and Europe. Don't you have anything normal? What about the Feilding Races? Then I could stop off at the farm and see my horse."

He looked embarrassed. "I know war stories are difficult for you, considering..."

Her lips tightened. Why did everyone bring that up? It had been almost two years.

"It's nothing to do with that. I just don't like to see Americans walking around as if they own the place."

"Tell you what," he said, forcing his lips into a facsimile of a smile. "Go up to Camp Russell and telephone me when you find out what the hell is going on. Then take a few days off to do whatever you want." He slapped the desk as an idea popped into his head. "Plus, you can take my car and keep it until Sunday night. You'd like that, wouldn't you?"

He pulled a key from his pocket and tossed it to her. She caught it in flight, grinning.

"So I can go home for a few days, see my horse, and go to the races if I stop off and find out what the US Marines are up to first? And I can take your Morris Roadster?"

"Yes, but don't drive it on grass if you can avoid it, I just had it polished. And no dogs as passengers. Also, if you visit your farm, bring me back some eggs. I haven't had an egg in over a year. Oh, and a pound of butter would be nice as well."

Her family farm had a few dairy cows and no hens. For the past year, most of the milk the farm produced had been sent to the Dairy Research Institute at Massey College in Palmerston North to be transformed into dehydrated butter for New Zealand troops fighting overseas. She'd be lucky to find a teaspoonful of butter, let alone a pound. Even margarine had recently disappeared from grocery shelves, shipped off to meet the growing demands of the troops fighting in the Pacific.

"I'll see what I can do," she promised. "Will I need to fill the petrol tank?"

"Depends on how far you drive. Have you got petrol coupons in your ration book?"

"My father gave me his. The Packard's sitting up at the farm because he has a driver now, but he still gets coupons. I'll pop off an article on the unfairness of petrol rationing if you like. That'll spark a few angry letters to the editor."

"Ring Mrs. Mason with the details," he said. "She can write it up. But please don't short-shrift the Marine camp. Spend as long as you can there. Prowl around a bit. I hate all this unnecessary secrecy. Have you ever driven a Roadster, by the way?"

She shrugged. "I'll ask the boys down in the garage for a quick lesson. Can't be much different from the Packard, and I drove that all the time before I moved to Wellington."

He stared at her through narrowed eyes, suddenly afraid for his prized Morris Oxford Roadster.

"Bring it back in one piece, Kate, or I'll have your guts for garters."

"Of course," she said breezily. "I'll drive slowly along the coast road with two hands on the steering wheel at all times, and I'll bring it back without a single chip on the paint, cross my heart."

She was speeding downhill on the winding gravel road from the highest point on Paekākāriki Hill when a man in a tan leather flight jacket zoomed past her on a dark red motorcycle, throwing up a cloud of dust and grit in his wake.

If he's dinged the paint on the Roadster, Max is going to kill me, she thought.

She hadn't heard him coming; the bike had appeared suddenly on the other side of the road, accompanied by a high, whining sound that rose and fell as he passed. Then he sped towards the next turn — still on the wrong side of the road.

She put her foot down, trying to catch up to him to alert him to what he was doing, but he was going too fast. He vanished around the curve, leaning the bike sideways with the pedal just above the surface of the road. God, if some poor sod was coming the other way, neither of them would have time to take evasive action. Fortunately, the hill road was usually empty, which is why she'd chosen that route — well, partly why. With petrol rationed, most cars sat up on blocks, wheels off, unused for the duration, and if the owners had to be somewhere, they took the more sedate and fuel-efficient coast road.

She heard the crash as she rounded the corner: a screech of rubber and the sound of a pedal being dragged across gravel, followed by a thump.

And sure enough, there he was, sitting in the ditch, apparently uninjured, his goggles pushed back onto his head, his motorcycle behind him leaning against a tree, its front wheel turned completely around but still spinning.

She slowed to a stop but kept the engine running. "Do you need help?"

He glared at her through oil-ringed eyes. "That bastard just forced me into the ditch. He was taking up the whole road."

An elderly man driving a tractor with a wagon load of hay behind had stopped and was staring at the man in the ditch, his mouth hanging open.

She caught the old man's eye and gave him a reassuring shrug.

"It was your bloody fault, you know," she said to the man in the ditch. She turned the car off and stepped out. "You were on the wrong side of the road, and he couldn't see you coming. I saw you go by and was sure you were going to crash into someone. You're lucky you didn't kill him."

He jumped out of the ditch and wrenched his bike away from the tree.

"I had this bike shipped from Hawaii at great expense, and look at the damn wheel now. Is there an Indian dealership nearby?"

An American, as she'd suspected. That was why he'd stayed on the wrong side of the road. Stories about Americans doing that were a thing of Kiwi legend.

"There's a mechanic at the garage down in Paekok," said the old man in heavily accented English. "He can fix all the engines. Trucks, tractors, motorcycles."

"Great. That'll do. We'll put my bike in your wagon, and you can take it to your guy. I'll follow with her."

"But I have my cows to milk," complained the old man.

The American ignored him, dragging his bike over to the wagon and wedging it between two bales of hay.

He came around to the passenger side of the Roadster and leaned on the door.

"Where are you headed, ma'am? Can you take me to Camp Russell after I speak to the mechanic? I can get you a couple of gallons of gas at the camp to cover the detour."

He'd rubbed some of the oil off his face with his shirtsleeve. Without the smears of oil on his cheeks and forehead, she could see he was quite good-looking, about thirty, maybe younger, tall, strongly built, with light brown, tousled hair and hazel eyes. Not that his appearance helped the situation. She wasn't in the mood for an American. On the other hand, she had wanted to find a way to get into the camp, and here was the solution presenting itself on a very attractive platter.

"I'm headed in that direction, but I have enough petrol, thanks. Consider it as me doing my part for the war effort." She gave him her best smile. "Lunch might be nice, though. I heard the meals are very good in the American canteens."

"See what I can do." He hopped into the front seat without using the door. "They aren't letting anyone in today, but I might be able to pull rank."

She went through the starting routine while he watched intently, probably suppressing the typical male desire to do it for her.

"Nice car," he said. "Yours?"

"It belongs to my boss."

She steered back onto the road. "Do you want me to go on ahead, or should I drive behind the tractor?"

"Drive behind the tractor so I can keep an eye on him," he said. "You don't happen to have a handkerchief, do you? I have oil in my eye."

"In my coat pocket. Help yourself."

He pulled out her best linen handkerchief and dabbed his eye, then stuffed it back into her pocket.

"Thanks for the assistance. Your War Office will be grateful." He held out his hand. "Major Harry Wilhelm of the U.S. Marine Corps, based out of our consulate in Wellington."

She released her grip on the steering wheel briefly and shook his hand.

"Kate Hardy."

"And how come you're driving north in this handsome car, Miss Hardy?"

"I'm visiting the family farm," she said. "And my boss said I could borrow his car."

He nodded and stared at the tractor through narrowed eyes.

"You'd think he could go faster than that."

Fifteen minutes later, she pulled up outside the only garage in Paekākāriki. He hadn't spoken a word since the handshake but had drummed his fingers on his knee impatiently while glaring at the tractor as it chugged along in front of them, belching smoke.

"I'll wait for you here."

"Sure."

Ten minutes later, he came out and flipped himself back into the passenger seat.

"Well?"

"He says he can fix it, but it'll take him the rest of the day. I expected that."

"So, to the camp then?"

He nodded. "If you wouldn't mind."

"Did you give the old man something for his trouble?"

"Yep. Five pounds. He seemed happy."

She started the car and tried to hide a smile.

"It was too much, wasn't it?"

"He would've been happy with five shillings. You gave him twenty times as much as that."

He shrugged. "He needs it more than I do. And you were right about it being my fault."

They drove towards the camp in silence. The wind had picked up, covering the ocean with white caps. She loved watching the movement of the waves, but along the shoreline, the water could be dangerous, with riptides and undertows and sudden drops in the ocean floor. At times, the wind was so strong you could lean into it and not fall. She could imagine a Japanese submarine running into trouble in the strait between Kapiti Island and the coast and beaching itself. Was that why he was going to the Marine camp? Was a submarine stuck out there?

In a few minutes, the entrance to the camp appeared between a line of trees. Two uniformed men came out of the gatehouse holding ferocious-looking Tommy guns pointed loosely in the direction of the car's grill. She itched to remind them that this was her country, not theirs, but the guns persuaded her to keep her mouth closed.

Major Wilhelm pulled a card from a pocket inside his jacket with two fingers and flashed it at one of the guards, who saluted. "Morning, sir, Major Wilhelm. We were told you were coming. Go right on through, sir."

He glanced over at Kate. "But no civilians, sir. Sorry, sir."

The major tucked the card back into his pocket. "She's with me," he said. "My driver. Can't leave her sitting outside the gates staring at her fingernails, can I? She can wait for me in the canteen. She won't see much in there."

"Wait there, please. I need to run it by the commandant."

The guard returned to the gatehouse and picked up a telephone, looking from Kate to the major and back as he spoke rapidly.

"Don't worry, they'll let you in," said the major. "You can sample the chocolate milkshakes and hamburgers in the canteen. I won't be more than an hour."

Kate was afraid to turn off the engine of the Roadster in case she couldn't start it again, so she left the engine running and kept her foot on the brake. The second guard lifted the gate suddenly, and she took her foot off the brake, then slammed it on again, jolting both of them forward; a Jeep driven by a uniformed man in dark sunglasses was coming out, and the guard had raised the arm for him. He took a good look at her as he drove slowly past and then gave a smiling thumbs up to Major Wilhelm.

Wilhelm shook his head, sighed audibly, and stared down towards the beach. Kate's foot was beginning to cramp with the effort of holding the brake on with her foot. What was the guard on the telephone talking about, for goodness sake?

Eventually, he put down the telephone and came out to the car.

"She can come in if she stays with you the whole time," he said to Wilhelm. "You're not to let her out of your sight."

She heard him say quietly under his breath, "Fuck." But he nodded his agreement.

As she pulled the car past the guards and through the gate, he said, "If you're going to stay with me the whole time, you'll need to know what's going on. And I hope you're not squeamish."

The thought of torture flashed through her mind. Surely, he hadn't been sent up here to interrogate someone or to beat something out of a poor captive. A Japanese prisoner of war, perhaps? She knew it happened. The Japanese prisoners in the POW camp on the other side of the ranges had rioted earlier this year, and several of them had been shot dead by the guards. Or could it be a Japanese submarine that had beached itself between the island and the coast, and the Marines had captured some of them?

"I can't watch any torture," she said.

"Torture? What makes you think of torture? No, nothing like that. Worse, in my opinion. I'm going to have to invoke the Official Secrets Act — yours — and the Espionage Act — ours. You have to swear that you won't tell anyone anything about what you're going to see or hear."

She nodded, her heart pounding. What the hell was she going to see that was worse than torture? And how could she not tell Max? She'd have to stay away from him for weeks to stop herself blabbing about it.

"We've been here training for Operation Cartwheel," he said.

"Forget that, by the way. Last night, thirty-five landing craft got stuck in the shallow water during a landing exercise. They were pulled off with a crane one at a time and towed back out to the escort ship — The *USS American Legion*. It took half the night, and the sea got pretty rough at the end. The last one was being pulled backward through ten-foot swells, and it flipped over. A dozen men went into the water dressed in heavy gear, many of them non-swimmers. Ten of them drowned. Bodies have been washing up on the beach ever since."

"Bodies? How many? Have they found all of them?"

"They've found ten bodies. That's the problem."

She was dying to pull out her notebook and start taking notes.

"What do you mean? Why is it a problem? Didn't ten men drown?"

"One man is still missing."

She frowned at him. "Ten drowned, ten found. I don't get it. How is one still missing?"

He stared at her for a minute through half-closed eyes as if deciding what to say.

"One of the bodies wasn't ours."

3

Bodies on the Beach

The wind whipped at Kate's coat as she walked along the beach, tearing it open and exposing her legs embarrassingly to the group of uniformed men who surrounded her. She thrust her hands into her pockets and pushed the two sides of the coat together but couldn't stop the hem from flipping up. She saw Major Wilhelm glance sideways at her legs a couple of times and wished she'd worn slacks.

As recently as 1939, no women wore slacks, but now they were working in factories and doing men's jobs, slacks had become commonplace. She'd written an article a few months ago about high school boys in Chicago wearing skirts to school as a protest against girls wearing slacks. The article generated plenty of angry letters to the editor, but all the women she spoke to were keen on the idea of abandoning skirts. No nylons, no long underwear in winter and fewer coupons needed. And, of course, no men staring at your legs when the wind caught your skirt.

The group reached the end of the beach, where a First Aid tent with a light dangling from the front pole had been erected high up on a pile of rocks.

"This is where they found him," said the camp commandant, Colonel Jackson. He was a plump middle-aged American with a thin David Niven mustache who was struggling to keep up with the group. "We haven't moved him. We thought you'd like to see him *in situ,* as it were."

The major nodded. "I would. He was up on the rocks, was he?"

"Yes, and well above the high tide mark, so he wasn't thrown up there by waves. He must have climbed up there on his own because ...." He stopped and glanced at Kate.

"She'll have to know everything," said the major. "I've impressed on her the importance of keeping this to herself."

"Come inside and take a look, both of you," said the commandant.

He opened the tent and gestured for Kate to go through ahead of him. She was feeling awkward about not mentioning she was a reporter but keen to see what was inside. So she smiled at him and stepped inside the tent where a tarpaulin had been tossed across the rocks. The smell hit her like a damp face cloth, and she pulled out her handkerchief to cover her nose. Not much use, as the hanky was smeared with oil, but the oil smelled better than whatever lay under the tarpaulin. She stood near the door to catch the salty gusts of wind from the ocean and took shallow breaths through her mouth.

"Are you okay?" asked Wilhelm. "If you need to faint, go back down to the beach."

She knew she was about to see a body. The smell wasn't just rotting seaweed or a dead seal. She'd seen dead animals before, but never a human body. But one thing she was sure of — she wasn't going to give Wilhelm the satisfaction of fainting, especially alone on the beach where he'd probably let her fall in a heap without running down to catch her.

"I'm fine," she said. "I grew up on a farm. I've seen death before."

It was the bodies of the Marines that had disturbed her the most, and she hadn't even seen them. They had passed nine wooden coffins laid across a newly-built platform on the way down from the camp. Two Marines in dress uniform stood at either end of the platform, heads bowed, right hands resting on the butts of rifles. Major Wilhelm stopped and saluted the coffins, then continued past the site. She'd felt a surge of anxiety and sorrow but had kept her head down until the coffins were well behind her. She had wanted desperately to wail and tear her hair out on their behalf. Imagine dying thousands of miles from home in icy waves, not storming an enemy stronghold, but merely training to do that. And they would all be young men — they always were.

"They're going to bury them at the McKay family cemetery, across the road from the camp," he said so quietly she could hardly hear him over the wind. "They're still searching for the missing man."

She stood near the door of the tent, her coat mercifully no longer blowing around, and watched as Major Wilhelm pulled back the tarpaulin, unable to stop herself from gasping as a body was exposed. The man was lying on his front, his face turned to one side, his arms splayed out as if he was in mid-fall. He had a wound on the back of his head that she was fairly sure was a bullet wound, even though it was quite small. What had shaken her more was that the man himself seemed familiar, somehow. Forgetting the smell, she stepped forward and crouched down to get a better look.

Wilhelm glanced at her. "Someone you know?"

"I'm not sure. Could you turn him over?"

Wilhelm raised his eyebrows at the commandant, who nodded. He slid his arm under the shoulders and rolled him on his back. One side of his face had gone where the bullet had exited, but she could see enough of him to be fairly sure she didn't recognize him, other than that, he looked like someone she might know. He was young, probably in his early twenties, like her, so she might have met him at a party in Wellington. But it was more of a feeling of familiarity than an actual recognition.

"A Scandi," she said after a minute. "I think he's a Scandi."

"Scandi? You mean Scandinavian?"

She nodded. "My grandmother is from Schleswig, on the border of Denmark and Germany, and this man looks like one of our people."

"So German, possibly?"

"Germans look different," she said. Did they, or was it just that she didn't want to think that they looked the same? She didn't know any Germans herself, but for various reasons, her family had always disliked them, and she found it difficult to be tolerant, especially since, early in the war, they'd sunk two ships off the coast of New Zealand, one of which had been carrying race horses.

The commandant leaned down to take a closer look at the face.

"Is he your man?"

Wilhelm frowned at him and nodded briefly. He already knew who it was but hadn't wanted her to know, she thought. Why was that? Her reporter's instincts were on high alert. A man who might be a German or a Scandinavian had been executed on this beach, right below an American military camp. Surely, executions didn't happen often in New Zealand. Since The Arms Act of 1920, all guns had to be registered at a police station, and semi-automatic weapons were banned entirely. In the last century, everyone had carried a gun, but since the last war, very few people did.

What was even stranger was that everyone at the camp, even the commandant, was deferring to Major Wilhelm as if he were the man in charge. Was that what he was? Had they called him in to identify the body or to work the case? And why wasn't he wearing a uniform? Was he working undercover? He'd introduced himself as a major.

Wilhelm returned the corpse to its original position and ran his hands down each side before sticking his hands in the man's pockets. The body was dressed in a khaki shirt and trousers — almost like a military uniform — but the shirt pocket had a red patch on it. Not anything she'd seen before, but something you might see on a prisoner or an asylum resident.

Major Wilhelm rose to his feet and gestured to an older man who had accompanied them down from the camp.

"Go ahead, doctor."

He strode out of the tent past Kate and stood at the entrance, staring out at the sea. He looked angry. He knew the victim but didn't want to say so in front of her.

The doctor knelt awkwardly beside the body and raised one arm.

"Been here awhile," he said. "Longer than a day, but not much longer. The body is relatively fresh."

"Before the accident," said the commandant. "And no one knew about that in advance. It just happened overnight."

Major Wilhelm had seemingly had enough of the commandant stating the obvious. He turned and glared at him and then said to Kate, "I've seen everything I need to. Let's go back to the camp and get lunch. Doctor, send your report down to Wellington as soon as you can. I'll be back here in a few days to discuss your findings."

She followed him to the Jeep that had brought them down. As he opened the door, the driver cupped his hand over his mouth and whispered in the major's ear.

The major glanced at Kate. "Thanks for looking into that, private. Drop us at the officers' mess."

"Closed today, sir."

"The enlisted men's canteen, then."

"I can take you to the P.X. There's a small canteen in the rear. It's the only place open today. Will that do?"

"I guess it will have to."

The Jeep raced up through the dunes and across the fields and stopped in front of a rickety building made of corrugated iron, raised above the ground on wooden blocks that she recognized as an old wool shed. The letters P.X. were painted above the door, and men were streaming in and out, clutching letters and parcels from home or goods unavailable to the locals, like bars of chocolate and silk stockings.

Kate waited until the major opened the door of the Jeep and climbed out.

"Do we need to have lunch?"

She was already thinking about what she would say to Max about the banned story she was witnessing. "I'm ready to leave, and I'm not hungry. I'll take you back to Paekākāriki, and you can get yourself lunch there if you like. I'd like to get to my family farm while it's still daylight."

He shook his head. "We need to discuss a couple of things."

He led her through the store and into an almost empty canteen, dragged out two chairs from a table, and sat in one of them. A uniformed man came from the kitchen, saluted, and waited for the major to speak first.

"Two chocolate shakes," said the major. "And a couple of hamburgers."

He wasn't going to give her a choice, convinced that she was so desperate for American food that she would jump at whatever he thought suitable.

"There's no cook here today, sir."

"Right. I forgot about that. How about lunch? Anything?"

"Sandwiches — ham or egg salad. And tea or coffee without milk. Or a nice cold Coca-Cola, of course."

He emphasized the word cold, which amused Kate. Why did Americans insist on putting ice in their drinks? And why did they always want beer from a fridge?

"I'd love a black coffee," she said. "Especially if it doesn't have chicory in it. And a ham sandwich." She hadn't tasted ham for months, and her mouth watered at the thought of biting into a sandwich made with real ham and not the kind that came in a tin. And she wasn't going to try a Coca-Cola. She'd seen people drinking it in Wellington, but it looked like molasses with bubbles. Black coffee was her drink of choice, a taste she'd picked up from her grandmother, who drank nothing else. She was still alive and kicking at eighty-eight, so it hadn't done her any harm.

"I'll have the same," said Wilhelm.

"Yesterday's bread," said the enlisted man apologetically.

The major shrugged.

"Fine."

As the enlisted man hurried off to make them coffee and a

sandwich, he said, "Tell me what you saw down there."

"A man who was either Scandinavian or German who was executed on the beach sometime before the drownings occurred," said Kate. "The killer used a short-barreled small calibre revolver if it was done close up. It would need to be close, considering where the body was found and that the entry wound wasn't very big. But still, probably fired at close range to hit him right in the back of his head. The short barrels aren't very accurate from further away."

The major raised his eyebrows. "You know about guns, then do you?"

"I grew up with guns," she said. "We used to do target practice on the farm, and I entered a few rifle shooting contests before the war and did well, even against men."

"Not much chance to practice since you moved to Wellington," he said, smiling slightly. "And started working as a reporter at *The Dominion*."

She avoided his eyes.

"How do you know about that?"

"I had you checked out while we were down on the beach."

"It was that easy?"

"I asked for the driver to put a call into the U.S. Consulate and run your name by them. Someone recognized the name Kate Hardy from an article you wrote recently. Something about the body of a woman being identified by her fingerprints. I took a chance it was you. Thanks for confirming that it was."

She stared down at the table so he couldn't see the relief in her eyes. He hadn't found out everything, then. Just as well. And he didn't seem curious about why she'd been assigned to write an article involving the police.

"I suppose you're not going to let me write about this, are

you?"

"Not a single word," he said. "Not about the drownings, not about the murder victim. Nothing. Nada. Zilch."

The sandwiches arrived, and she bit into hers. Real ham, with butter and mustard, and a cup of the best coffee she'd tasted since the war began. This was why she had to use a ration book — so the US Marines could feast on the best food available in the country.

"Could I at least tell my editor about the drownings? He knows he's not allowed to publish certain things, but he'll just keep pushing to find out if I don't tell him something."

"I'll have the consulate give him a call. If they permit him to write about the accident, that's all he can write about. The murder must remain under wraps. Don't mention the murder victim, either."

"You recognized the man, didn't you? Who was he?"

He bit into his sandwich. "Can't say."

She frowned at him. "No? But you thought he looked German. Are you looking for a spy? A German spy in New Zealand? Surely, there aren't any German spies here. It's the Japanese we're worried about. I'd hate to be a person of Japanese ancestry in this country. The Japanese air force has been bombing Darwin for more than a year, and they've even been into Sydney Harbour. If Australia falls, we won't have a chance. People here are very nervous about a Japanese invasion."

That's why Max always makes me write about the Women's Institute, she wanted to add. To keep women's minds calm.

"The Japs are not going to invade Australia. Not now."

"My father thinks they might."

"Why would he know?"

"Just an educated guess on his part," she said quickly. "Why would you know, for that matter?"

He grinned. "Chester Nimitz is a buddy of mine."

"You win."

"Seriously, though. The Japanese are looking more to the Pacific north of Australia. They're worried about us at this point, and they'd like to know how many Marines are training in New Zealand and what our plans are for invasion in the Pacific. They need eyes and ears here, and Germans already embedded in the community would be useful. Japanese are harder to conceal."

"The government has interned hundreds of Germans," said Kate. "On Somes, the quarantine island in Wellington Harbour. I don't like it, personally. If you're born here of German ancestry, does that mean you'll be loyal to Germany? I don't believe so. And what about people like my grandmother? She was born in what was Germany at the time. She speaks German and Danish, but she thinks of herself as Danish. She hates Germans. And yet, after the First World War, she had to register as an enemy alien, which just about killed her. If my grandfather had been alive, he would have wanted to kill someone for that."

"Can't take a chance with loyalty," he said. "Although I don't suppose your grandmother's a risk. How old is she?"

"Nearly ninety," admitted Kate. "She came from Schleswig in 1874, ten years after the Second Schleswig War, so she's been here most of her life. She settled in what was called the Seventy Mile Bush with other Scandinavians, and they've married into other immigrant groups. My grandfather came here with the British Army, so she's lucky she has a British surname. But people are tough on anyone with a German-sounding name. They've smashed windows of shops, and a relative of mine had a brick thrown through the window of his house, even though he fought in the last war. They get spat on sometimes, even long-time residents, and the government even opens their mail."

"Hmm," he said. "On the other hand, I've heard that German nationals trying to avoid internment are hiding in Scandinavian communities. What do you know about that?"

"Maybe they are, but they must be terrified," she said. "How would you like to be sent to a camp away from friends with no end in sight just because you're of German ancestry or even a recent immigrant? And who knows how long the war will last? They could be interned for years. Everyone thought the last war would be over in a few weeks, but they know better this time."

He shrugged. "Can't be helped. We're doing it back home as well. That's what happens in wartime."

"What about you? You have a German name. Is it difficult for your family in America?"

"No. But I've been in Hawaii for years. My family would suffer in silence. They wouldn't ask me for help."

"Sounds like my family. Well, if you've grilled me enough, I'd like to get going. I want to see my horse before it gets dark. I haven't seen her in over a month, and I have a three-hour drive ahead of me."

He stood up. "Let's go then. I don't want to keep you from your horse."

She drove him back down the hill to Paekākāriki and pulled up outside the garage.

"I'll wait, just in case."

He gave her a half-wave and went inside the garage. When he came out ten minutes later, he was wheeling his red motorcycle.

He stood it up with the kickstand, came over to the roadster, and held out his hand.

"Thanks for everything."

He held her hand longer than he should have, his eyes locked on hers as if he were trying to work something out. She could feel a red wave coming up her neck but kept her eyes on his. Finally, he grinned and let her go.

"See you around sometime, maybe."

"It's a small country," she said defensively.

She watched as he started the motorcycle with a kick and roared up towards the highway. He was heading north, by the look of it. Or perhaps, like her, he preferred the rush of returning to Wellington by the hill road.

She followed his dust up to the main road, but by the time she got there, he'd vanished along the asphalt road, leaving no hint of his direction.

The sun set shortly after five in June, and she had no idea how to turn on the headlights. The boys at the garage had forgotten to mention that detail. She needed to get a move on.

She put her foot down and headed towards the farm, hoping the cold wind would cool her anger and whatever else it was that was making her feel so flustered and not herself.

4

Palmerston North

Kate made the distance from Camp Russell to the family farm in record time, unable to stop herself from speeding even as the setting sun blinded her. It was dark when she finally reached the farm and drove through the gate that led into the lower paddock. Racehorses had once been kept in the lower paddock, but now it was the site of a Victory Garden. She often thought about what it must have been like back when her grandparents had first moved here. She would have loved to have lived back then. Granny had told her stories about those times her entire life. Mostly the fun, adventurous parts, although sometimes, when she was feeling sad about Granddad, she would tell a sad story.

A lamp was glimmering in the small cottage where Betty and Tom, the couple who helped on the farm, lived. She could see their shadows against the curtains as they cleared the table from their evening meal. They were English and had come to New Zealand before the war. Tom, who had been injured in the last war, walked with a slight limp and relied on his younger, dark-haired wife for help. Granny had hired them because she felt sorry for Tom, but she hadn't regretted her decision. He was quite capable of milking the dairy cows and driving the old truck over to Massey College loaded with butter. And he kept the electric fences in good shape so no wild animals could get in.

"No wild dogs will get into my property," Granny had declared when she became one of the first farmers in the district to install the new electric fences. Kate couldn't remember ever seeing a feral dog, and there were no other predators in the country bigger than a possum, but Granny could do what she wanted with her money.

As she glided by the cottage, trying not to make too much noise with the car, she saw the shadows converge. They were having a romantic moment.

That decided her. She couldn't take her horse out without disturbing them, and if she went into the stable, they would hear sounds and come out to investigate. At that point, it was almost too dark to ride anyway. She was disappointed, but she could see her horse in the morning. Betty would have exercised her; she adored Southern Cross.

She navigated the narrow lane up to the house, wincing at the sound of branches scraping along the side of the Roadster. No lights other than the reflected pink glow of the setting sun from her old bedroom window. No Granny — turning on the outside light was part of her routine, and she certainly never sat inside in darkness. She had gone somewhere, but for how long? And had she taken the car?

Granny still drove, but only during the day and only into Palmerston North or Feilding to visit friends. Kate's father had been trying to discourage her from getting behind the wheel since before the war, but he was too busy these days to take the time.

"If she gets into an accident and kills herself, well, she's nearly ninety, and she's had a good life. She's probably looking forward to being with Dad again anyway."

Kate also had her doubts about her elderly grandmother driving. What if she ran someone over? She claimed to have perfect eyesight, and perhaps she did, but her reactions had slowed in the past three or four years, and the steering wheel of the Packard needed some strength to turn, not like the Roadster, which Kate could steer with one hand.

The Packard was usually kept in the barn on the other side of the farm with the dairy cattle because that part of their property exited directly onto the road to Feilding; she thought about checking to see if it was gone, but if it had it wouldn't prove anything because it was clear Granny wasn't home. She parked the Roadster in front of the house, unlocked the front door, and turned on all the downstairs lights. She'd heard so many stories over the years about what had gone on at this farm she felt nervous being here alone. Wild dogs were one thing, but Granny had told her that at least two killers had visited the farm, and once, she had shot at a woman herself who was about to kill Grandpa. Sometimes, it seemed that Granny and Granddad had lived in an adventure novel and not in real life.

The refrigerator was empty, and so was the bread bin. She opened one of the jars of peaches from the pantry and ate half of them with two of Granny's homemade ginger nut biscuits she found in a tin beside the bread bin. At least she wouldn't starve. A girl could live a long time on bottled peaches and ginger nuts.

Next time she decided to come up here at the last minute, she would telegraph Granny to say she was on her way.

She woke before dawn and gobbled down the rest of the peaches and two more ginger nuts. She was torn between ringing Granny's friends or going down to the stable and visiting her horse. The horse won out. Granny could wait.

She'd owned Southern Cross since before the war, a beautiful chestnut Thoroughbred that Granny had given her for her twenty-first birthday. The farm had once been a stud farm, but now hers was the only horse in the stable. Tom and Betty took good care of her, and Betty rode Southern Cross so much that Kate was a little anxious that her horse would not be there.

And just as she thought, the horse was gone. A faint line of dust hovering around the gate hinted that they had left recently.

The day stretched before her with no food, no horse, and no one to talk to. She rang Granny's best friend Grace, who lived in an old people's home in Wellington, but failed to make herself understood; Grace yelled into the telephone while holding it at arm's length, claiming she couldn't hear and telling Kate to speak up. Eventually, a nursing assistant took the telephone from Grace and confirmed that Granny had not visited for some time.

A quick trip down the hill to the dairy farm showed that the Packard was missing, so Granny had driven off somewhere on an overnight trip. That was odd but not impossible. She could have left the car in town and taken the train somewhere.

The Roadster was sitting in front of the house, reminding her of the previous day. Had the major returned to Wellington and contacted Max, or just rung the American Consulate and had them make the call? And who was the man they'd seen dead on the beach? Major Wilhelm seemed to think he was German and believed Germans might be hiding inside Scandinavian communities. Palmerston North still had a large Scandinavian community, and most of them attended the Lutheran Church. She had the key to the car in her trouser pocket, and without taking time to think about it, she hopped into the car and started it up.

She would ask the pastor of the Lutheran Church, Rev. Christensen, if he knew of any Germans who were new to town, and — she knew it was unlikely — she might even see Major Wilhelm looking for whomever it was he was hoping to find. She felt a little buzz of excitement at the thought of seeing him again. Damn American, pushing himself into her thoughts like that.

The Reverend was busy with a funeral, however, and she knew when it was over, he would follow the cortege to the Palmerston North Cemetery along with the mourners. Kate stood at the back of the church and scanned the group of parishioners — the Knudsens, the Sorensens, the Nissens, the Clausens, the Mortensens — she had known them all her life. She could see no one in the pews who looked remotely like a German spy.

She left and walked back across the Square to where she'd parked the Roadster in front of Collinson & Cunninghame. Before the war, eons ago, she'd bought her winter coats there, but now she had to consider whether she had enough coupons. A sign in the window suggested that she should be careful using the latest issue of coupons because the store would have some 'lovely things to offer for the new season' in August and September. Even 'Hitler wouldn't undermine the quality,' the sign asserted. Her lips twitched. Thank heavens Hitler wasn't targeting the quality of women's coats. That would be beyond the pale.

Still smiling, she crossed the railway tracks that ran down the center of the Square and went over to the Royal Hotel. Granny had told her that the first time she saw Granddad, he had been sitting on the front steps of the hotel but hadn't looked at her. After he died, Granny had an opportunity to buy the hotel, and she still owned it, as well as several other buildings facing onto the Square. She visited the hotel often to rekindle the past. Perhaps she was there now. She had a permanent room available to her.

A large grassy paddock used for guests to park cars filled the space beside the hotel, and Kate decided she would look for Granny's car there. The Packard was very recognizable, and there were only a dozen cars parked in the paddock.

No sign of the car, but a motorcycle was propped on its stand beside a cabbage tree in the center. A motorcycle very much like the one Major Wilhelm had been driving. Her heart jumped a little. Could he be staying at the Royal Hotel? Was that his motorcycle?

She couldn't tell from the street, so she opened the gate, keeping an eye out for him, half expecting him to come out and sit on the veranda. She had felt as if she was being watched since she drove into the Square, and she'd hate him to find her looking at his bike.

The bike was covered in mud, making it hard to tell what color it was, although she thought she could see a hint of red on the front mudguard. He'd said something about an Indian dealer when she met him on the road, which must mean the bike was an Indian. She squatted beside it and ran her fingers over the rear mudguard, hoping to find a nameplate, but it was smooth. She took out her handkerchief, spat on it, and rubbed away at the front mudguard. Nothing showed it was an Indian motorcycle. More red paint, though. It must be his. Where was he, then? Staying at the hotel? And what was he doing in

Palmerston North? The town was not on a main route north or even the main road that ran from Wellington through the Gorge.

She folded the handkerchief and twisted herself around to stuff it into her trouser pocket. When she turned back to the bike, he was leaning on the seat, smirking down at her. She stared back at him, almost afraid to breathe. Blast. Caught in the act.

* * *

Harry had left the Marine Corps Paekākāriki unsure of what his next move should be. He'd asked his driver at the camp to call the consulate and see if they knew a woman named Kate Hardy, and they'd come up with someone of that name who may or may not be the Kate Hardy he'd met on the road. He wasn't sure. Wellington hadn't seemed like a large city, so chances were they had the right one. She'd admitted to being Kate Hardy, the reporter, but she'd refused to look at him when he said he'd checked her out. Something wasn't right with her.

He worried about how convenient it was she happened to come along right after a farmer with a German accent pulled his hay wagon into his path, causing him to spin his bike into the ditch. At the time, Harry had been sure the whole thing was a setup, but he'd been relieved when the consulate knew of Kate Hardy, the reporter.

Then again, if it was a setup, they'd send a good-looking woman, and they certainly knew his type — tall, slim, thick, wavy hair. She'd been cagey, though; there was something she wasn't telling him. So, time to call it in, that and the confirmation of the identity of the victim. No use calling the consulate. He needed to go directly to the top — the Security Intelligence Bureau, the New Zealand version of the Office of Strategic Services. His superiors in Hawaii had worked with the S.I.B. to coordinate his mission, and the man in charge had given his approval. Not that he'd had much choice. Everyone had to kowtow to the Americans these days if they wanted to win the war.

Yes, he definitely needed to find out if they'd heard of her at the S.I.B.

He'd been heading south along the coast road, returning to Wellington, so he pulled over and turned back towards Camp Russell. He needed to make a telephone call, and he needed to make it in a place where absolutely nobody could overhear him, especially not an operator or a nosy woman on a party line. Even the camp telephones might not all be secure. He'd have to use the commandant's private line.

The commandant was enjoying a shot of whiskey in the officer's mess and did not look happy to see Harry.

"You're back," he said, continuing his habit of stating the obvious.

"I am, and I need to use your telephone ASAP."

"There's one in the back room you can use. Lift the receiver and tap on ..."

"No good. I need a secure line. Do you have a secure line in your office?"

The commandant tossed back his whiskey and dragged himself reluctantly to his feet.

"Yeah. Follow me."

In his office adjacent to the mess, he gestured towards a rotary phone on the desk.

"Use that one. Tap on the cradle to get the camp telephone operator, and he'll put you through. He'll know it's coming from this telephone, and I alerted him to your presence earlier. Give him your name and rank, and he'll make the call for you." He sat down on the edge of his desk and looked at his watch, sighing loudly.

"No sign of the last body," he said. "My men are still searching..."

Harry paused, his hand hovering above the telephone cradle. "I need you to leave, colonel. I have a highly secretive call to make."

"Where to? It's not an overseas call, I hope. You'll need to reserve that at least ten hours in advance, maybe more. This country is backward with its telephony."

"Nope. In country. Can't say where, I'm afraid. Could you close the door on your way out, please?"

The commandant strode from the room, his retreating back stiffly conveying his displeasure at being treated like an enlisted man.

Harry tucked the phone under his chin and tapped the cradle; the operator answered immediately, his salute coming at Harry through the wires.

"Sir?"

"This is Major Wilhelm in the commandant's office. Put me through to Wellington 41-073 if you would."

"Right away, sir."

He heard a series of clicks, and a voice said, "Captain Bates speaking."

"Major Wilhelm calling from Camp Russell," said the operator. "Putting you through now."

"Wilhelm? What have you found out? Was it our man from

the internment camp?"

Harry waited a couple of beats for the operator to disconnect.

"Yep. Shot in the back of the head, execution-style."

"Dammit. Poor bastard. Anything on the body to indicate what went down?"

"Nothing in particular. I don't believe it was connected to the Marine camp, but they have investigators looking into it and a doctor doing an autopsy. Doubt they'll find anything, though. And they won't figure out who he was. He hasn't been here long."

"Was he dumped there? Or was he taken down and executed on the beach?"

"Executed on the spot. He was lying face down on rocks, well above the high tide mark. I'm guessing the killer assumed he'd be taken away by the tide, so he's probably not a local man. Brought here because they thought it was far enough from where they met him to avoid easy identification. The killer's luck ran out when the landing craft overturned, the beach was searched, and the commandant thought to call you about it. He could have rotted there for a while."

"It would have made more sense to dump him on the East Coast, though, don't you think? Lots of empty beaches over there. And why leave him on the beach? Why not throw him in the water?"

"I've been wondering about that. Why this beach? Was he trying to throw suspicion on the Marines? Was someone sending us a message?"

Or was the killer a Marine? Harry wasn't going to put that idea into Bates's head. If he was a Marine, the U.S. Military Police would have to deal with it, and they'd want it kept from the locals.

"What are your next steps, then?"

"I'm going back to the source at the internment camp to find out what happened right after his group escaped. Where they went. Then I'm going to do a run through the Scandinavian and German communities north of the internment camp to see if I can spot any of the others hiding out."

"Be careful. Don't get yourself killed. Do you have a weapon?"

"Not allowed to carry one, can't get a permit," said Harry. "But I have a knife. I can take care of myself. Hell, I survived on Guadalcanal without any sleep for weeks, and our weapons were almost useless in the mud and rain."

"Why the Scandinavian towns? Why not German communities?"

"Two reasons. The towns to the north of the internment camp were mostly settled by Scandinavians, and it would be easy for the fugitives to disappear into those communities. They'd fit right in."

"You might be right. I hadn't thought of that. Of course, they could be anywhere in New Zealand by now. What was your second point?"

"I had an accident today that I suspect might not have been an accident. An old German farmer drove his wagon into my path and knocked me off my bike; I was picked up almost immediately by a young woman who claimed to be a reporter but also mentioned that she had German ancestry and disliked the internment of German citizens. Said her grandmother came from the Danish-German border."

There was a long silence from the other end, and then the man said slowly, "Not Kate Hardy, I hope."

"What? Yes, it was. She's a legitimate reporter, I guess, but...

"

"Stay away from Kate Hardy."

"Can you tell me why?"

"No, I can't, but she's not part of any conspiracy, I can assure you. Keep away from her, seriously, Harry. You'll get yourself in trouble."

"O.K. If you insist. She said she was heading to her farm, but she didn't tell me where it was. Do you know? I'd hate to bump into her accidentally."

"Off the Awahuri Road, up near Feilding," said the man on the phone, missing the true point of Harry's question. "It isn't a Scandinavian community, so you have no reason to go there, and I doubt you'd run into her accidentally if that's what you're intending. Don't go anywhere near Feilding, Harry, please."

"Where should I start then?"

"Palmerston North has a large Scandinavian community. From there, go through the Manawatu Gorge to Woodville and head north. Norsewood, Dannevirke, you'll be able to tell by the names. Look at some of the smaller villages as well."

"Palmerston North, then," said Harry. "I'll call you in a few days."

"And make sure it isn't just a regular murder. I don't want to look like a fool like my predecessor. You know that story, do you?"

Harry knew the story well. He'd heard it way too many times. The head of the S.I.B. had listened to a fantasist who'd walked in off the street claiming he'd been approached by the Nazis and asked to join a cell of saboteurs who were dropped off by a German submarine on the coast up north. Why he'd believed that no one knew.

"What happened to him?" asked Harry. He hadn't heard that

part of the story.

"When everything came out, he was sent back to England in disgrace. I took over, but now I have to answer to the Wellington Constabulary. Bloody nuisance. The Superintendent is constantly on my case, asking where things stand. He's very keen to know what you're doing, so make sure it's solid."

"I'm pretty sure this is real," said Harry. "They killed my guy, and it wasn't random. I'm going after them. We thought there was a cell embedded in this area, and now I'm sure of it. I intend to track them down and bring them in."

Starting with Kate Hardy, he thought. Insisting he should stay away from her had guaranteed he would do the opposite. He needed to find out what she was up to and why S.I.B. didn't want him near her.

Besides, there were those legs. Worth taking another look at those.

He had an old road map of the North Island in his saddlebag, and he spread it out on his knee. There it was. Awahuri, ten miles north of Palmerston North. Convenient. He'd go to Palmerston North, get a room for the night, and find her farm tomorrow. He'd give it a day, then ride through the Gorge to Pahiatua and see what the folks living in sight of the camp could tell him.

He wouldn't go inside the camp itself as it was probably packed with Nazi sympathizers ready to pass on details of what he looked like to outside interests.

He'd spoken to the commandant of the internment camp, Major Perrett, at length by telephone and had learned everything he needed to know about the escape. One of the men had set fire to a workshop, and while the guards and the local volunteer fire brigade were attempting to put it out, several men had gone over the fence. Perrett had intended to improve the fence and build a special compound for high-risk internees, but he hadn't had time to do it. He promised to close the barn door right away now that the horses had left.

Captain Bates at the S.I.B. had wanted to bring in Major Perrett and grill him about the escape. Perrett had been transferred to the internment camp after overseeing the rapid construction of the Japanese P.O.W. camp in Featherston, a few miles south of Pahiatua. He was a tough, resourceful man with an impeccable military reputation, and the new head of the S.I.B. had insisted that he was above suspicion. Harry was inclined to agree.

He was finishing breakfast at his hotel, seated at a table by the window, when he heard the throaty roar of a sports car. He flipped back the curtain, and there she was, speeding past him in the Roadster.

Well, that saved him from having to track her down at her family farm.

He tossed down the last inch of coffee and ran down the front steps just as she disappeared around a corner in a swirl of dust. He sprinted in the direction she had gone and discovered it was a dead-end street leading to a church. He watched from behind a tree as she went into the church. The number of cars parked along the street indicated that something was going on at the church, and after a few minutes, he heard the sound of a familiar hymn wafting towards him. He hadn't attended church since he was a boy, but his grandparents made sure he went every Sunday, and some of the songs had stuck in his head ever since, transporting him back to his childhood. Had to be either a wedding or a funeral. The hymn pointed to a funeral.

He returned to the hotel and waited for her next move in a

shaded area on the veranda. Within twenty minutes, she drove back into the Square, parked the car outside a department store, and spent ten minutes staring at coats in the window.

He was thinking about going inside and ordering another cup of weak coffee when she spun around and started walking in his direction, her eyes fixed on the spot where he'd left his bike. Damn. He'd been outed.

He ran back inside to the breakfast room.

"Is there a back door in this hotel?" he asked the waitress, a young country girl who went bright red every time he glanced in her direction. He couldn't blame her. The shortage of men in the town was noticeable. She probably hadn't exchanged words with a man under forty since the start of the war.

"You can go through the kitchen, but it just leads to the car parking area. You could just as easily go through the front door to reach your car if that's where...."

Harry dropped a shilling on the table. "Thanks. That's for you."

She picked up the coin and looked at it in the palm of her hand as if he had just given her a bouquet of roses. Not used to tipping in this country, he'd discovered. What the hell? He was going to tip whether they liked it or not.

He walked briskly through the kitchen and out the back door, ignoring the cook's protests.

Kate Hardy was squatting beside his bike, rubbing off the layer of dust that it had acquired when he drove over a dirt road to reach town.

What was she up to? Did she think he was concealing something on his bike? Wait. The color had been muted by the dust. She was making sure it was his. He hadn't seen any other Indian motorcycles since he landed in Wellington a few weeks ago, and definitely no red ones.

She had her back to him, so he walked quietly across the grassy area and around the front of the bike just as she turned to put something in her pants pocket. She was wearing a gold-colored tweed jacket with a brown velvet collar over a cream silk blouse, her hair falling forward over her cheek. Maureen O'Hara, he thought suddenly. That's who she looked like. Maureen O'Hara, only with darker hair. He'd seen her in a movie about the Marines back on the base in Oahu: *The Shores of Tripoli*. After they saw the movie, half the men on the base pinned her photograph on their lockers. He preferred Rita Hayworth, but Maureen O'Hara was pretty easy on the eyes.

He stepped around her to the other side of the bike and waited.

She turned around and looked up at him, her face slowly turning pink. Was it guilt or something else?

He leaned on the seat and grinned down at her.

"Looking for something?"

She stared at him, her mouth opening and closing like a goldfish, unable to explain herself.

He grabbed her arm and hoisted her to her feet.

"Let's go into the hotel and have a discussion. I'm sure you have a few questions, and so do I."

5

Kate and Harry at the Royal Hotel

She wanted to wrench her arm away, but at the same time, she liked the feel of his warm hand gripping her elbow. How could she explain what she had been doing and why? She went on the attack.

"Have you been following me?"

"Why would I want to do that?"

She had no answer for that. She could hardly accuse him of wanting to get to know her better; he was holding her arm as if he thought she might make a run for it and making no attempt to charm her.

She shrugged. He could take what he liked from that.

"Maybe you've been following me," he said, grinning down at her, revealing beautifully straight American teeth. Were they all born with teeth like that? New Zealanders had the worst teeth in the world. More than one woman she knew had had all her teeth removed and replaced with false teeth. Thank goodness Granny had made sure she kept her teeth in good condition. Imagine trying to kiss someone with false teeth. And why had she even thought that?

She'd have to stop noticing every little thing about him, she thought. He wasn't that good-looking, and he was too bossy for her taste. And an American. She'd already decided she wasn't ready for an American right now, no matter how nice his teeth were.

"What? No. Of course, I haven't," she said. "This is where I live. Palmerston North, I mean."

"I thought you lived on a farm?"

"My family farm is ten miles from here. I went to visit my grandmother, but she wasn't home, and there was nothing to eat, so I came into town to shop for food. I told you I was visiting my family farm."

"Yeah, you did. I saw you coming out of the Lutheran church a few minutes ago, and I heard hymns. Got some family in there today?"

He had been following her. That was why he'd accused her of following him, to throw her off balance in case she'd seen him.

"If you must know, there was a funeral going on, and I thought I'd check to see if there were any strangers in there — especially any Germans I didn't know. But I knew them all. Not a single spy among them."

He nodded slowly. "So you know all the Scandinavians in town, and you'd recognize a stranger? Look, that's why I'm here. To find someone hiding in your community. Have a drink with me, and we'll talk about it."

"It's too early for a drink, but I do need to eat. All I've had today is bottled peaches."

"Bottled? You mean canned, I guess. Yeah, I'll buy you lunch if you like."

He kept hold of her arm as they went up the steps to the Royal Hotel and into the bar as if he expected her to bolt suddenly.

Once they were inside the hotel, he released his hold.

"Where do they serve lunch? In the breakfast room?"

"In the pub. Follow me."

A young Asian man was washing glasses behind the bar, and he grinned at Kate.

"G'day, Kate. Bit early for you, isn't it?"

She gestured at the major with her head.

"My mate here is going to buy me lunch. What's on the menu?"

"Cottage pie," he said. "That's all I have. Unless you want liver and onions, I could do that for you. With mashed potatoes. Wouldn't take long."

"Mince and liver aren't rationed yet," she said to the major. "The liver and onions dinner is pretty good if you don't want the pie."

"I'll just have a beer," he said. "Whatever you have on tap."

"Cottage pie for me, please, Benny. And a glass of fizzy water."

He pulled out a chair for her at a table near the bar. She sat down and leaned on her elbows. She could still feel the warmth of his hand on her arm, even though he'd released it as they came through the door.

"Well, what do you want to know?"

He sat opposite her and leaned forward.

"Tell me your life story."

"Nothing to tell. I was born in England at the end of the war. My father was there with the army. My mother was English, died when I was a baby, and I was mostly brought up by my grandmother. She lives on the farm, and she taught me how to ride, shoot, and garden. All kinds of useful things."

"She taught you how to shoot? What is she, Annie Oakley?"

Kate laughed. "She can't shoot herself, but she spent so much time with my grandfather that she feels as if she's an expert."

"I grew up with my grandparents," he said. "My grandmother was an excellent cook, but I didn't learn a damn thing from her. I can boil an egg, and that's about it."

"You said they were German, originally. Can you speak German?"

He smiled at her. "*Ja, mein Schatz.*"

She looked down at her hands, her cheeks turning pink.

"I can speak some German as well, and I know what that means."

"In that case, you probably know it's a term of endearment," he said. "That's what my grandmother used to call me."

"*Min skat,*" she said. "That's what it is in Danish."

"Well, *min skat,*" he said. "Where's Benny with my beer?"

"He's coming from behind the counter with a tray of drinks right now."

"Who's Benny, and how do you know him?"

"He's the grandson of my grandmother's best friend, Grace Li."

Benny brought the beer and a glass of fizzy water for Kate.

"Here you go. Food's coming right up."

The major picked up the beer and took a small sip, watching her over the rim.

"So he's been in New Zealand for a while?"

She wasn't going to let him think that Benny was one of his damn spies. Benny's brother was fighting in Italy, and the only reason Benny was here was because he'd had polio as a child and was lame in one leg. Surely, he'd seen Benny limping.

"Born here. And his parents were born here. I've known him my whole life. Our grandmothers started a business together in Palmerston North more than fifty years ago. A shoe shop."

"I'm not accusing him of being a spy. I lived in Hawaii for years, and I like the combination of Japanese, Chinese, and Polynesian cultures you find there. Makes a place more interesting to have different ethnic groups. Better food as well."

"Were you there during the attack?"

He nodded. "I was at the Marine Barracks. We weren't attacked directly, but we fired at the Japs from the Parade ground. We hit a couple of them, but it was all over pretty quickly."

"You were safe, though," she said. "And after that, where did you go when your president declared war?"

He shrugged. Different places. I was in Guadalcanal with the Second Division Raiders for a bit. Then, I was sent here for a mission. I'll be off to another battle before the end of the year. Somewhere in the southern Pacific. No idea where, exactly."

She felt a wave of disappointment. He was only here for a few months then. Well, as long as he was here, he was safe, and maybe the war would end soon. One could always hope.

He took a swig of his beer.

"Tell me more about your grandmother's shop. What made her open a shoe store?"

"New Zealand came out of a recession right at the time she met her friend Grace — the mid-eighties, I think. New Zealand started sending frozen meat to England, and everyone was better off, so her timing was perfect. Shoes are a luxury, you know. Good shoes, anyway. She and Grace ended up with a chain of shops in all the larger cities. Jensen and Li, you may have seen the Wellington shop. They sold the chain before the war and made a fortune from the deal."

"Huh. And your grandfather owned the farm where she still

lives?"

"He was given land after the Māori Wars, and he went into stud farming. He knew everything about horses, and he bred some wonderful racers, but he never managed to make any money. Granny was already pretty well off from her shops when he died after the Great War, and she's been buying property ever since."

"What kind of property?"

Benny laid a dish of cottage pie in front of her, and she dug in. Wilhelm kept sipping his beer, waiting for her to answer, and eventually, she told him. "This hotel, for one."

He was silent for a few minutes, then said, "I'll tell you who I'm looking for, and we can take a walk around town afterward so you can show me the places where Scandinavians hang out."

"Alright then. But other than the Lutheran Church, there isn't anywhere that's mostly Scandinavians. They're just regular citizens now, you know, and they blend in. Quite a few of the older families live up in Stoney Creek and Bunnythorpe. My grandmother's sister used to live in Bunnythorpe."

He put down his beer. "Do you know a place called Pahiatua?"

She nodded. "On the other side of the Gorge. My Uncle Hamlet lives just outside of town. He has a stud farm beside the race track. My grandmother might be visiting him, now I think of it. They're very close."

A look crossed his face that she couldn't interpret.

"Do you know about the internment camp there?"

"You mean for Germans? No, I thought the internment camp was on Somes Island in Wellington Harbour."

"Yeah, but the internees were moved up to Pahiatua earlier this year because work needed to be done on Somes. They're using the race course to house them."

"The race course? It wouldn't be as secure as Somes Island, would it?"

"No, as it turned out, it wasn't. A group of men escaped, and we haven't found most of them."

"Except for one," she said, guessing. "The body we saw on the beach."

"What makes you think that?"

"The commandant at the Marine Corps camp asked if it was your man, and you said he was. What did you mean? Was he working for you?"

"Not directly, but I worked with him. He was put on Somes to keep an eye on things. Some questionable men had already attempted to escape, and we wanted to make sure we knew about any further escapes they might be planning."

"So you think one of the other fugitives could have killed him? If so, why would his body be on Kapiti Coast?"

He shrugged. There was more to it than he was saying, Kate thought. She was about to grill him about who, specifically, he was looking for, which he hadn't told her, when the door was flung open, and an older couple entered, a tall, slender elderly woman in a long mauve coat and smart black patent leather boots, her white gold hair wrapped around her head in tight braids, and a portly man with a shock of white hair and a bristly white mustache.

Kate leaped to her feet and flung her arms around the woman. "Granny! I'm so happy to see you. And Uncle Hamlet as well. I came home to the farm yesterday and was so disappointed you weren't there."

Major Wilhelm had risen to his feet and was standing behind her.

"Major Wilhelm, this is my uncle — well, my second cousin,

really — Hamlet Sorensen, the one with the horse farm in Pahiatua. And this is my grandmother, Mette Hardy."

The major shook hands with Hamlet, who asked, "Is that your Scout Indian motorcycle outside? Magnificent thing. I'd love to chat with you about it sometime."

"Sure. Take it for a spin now if you like. I can wait."

Wilhelm turned his attention to the older woman, who took both his hands in hers, smiled warmly up at him, and asked, "Are you Kate's new boyfriend? You remind me so much of my Frank."

Before Kate had a chance to deny that the major was her new boyfriend, Granny turned to her and asked, "What would Brian have to say about this?"

For a minute, she could hardly breathe.

6

Kate Goes to Pahiatua

They were sitting uncomfortably close on the steps of the hotel, Wilhelm with one booted foot resting on his knee, his arm draped along the step behind her back, watching Hamlet take a turn around the Square on the motorcycle. She was afraid to move in case she accidentally brushed against him.

"So who's Brian?" he asked suddenly.

"I don't want to talk about him," said Kate. "I'm sorry, but he's off limits."

"In the army?"

She ignored him and watched Uncle Ham steer the Indian awkwardly around the Square, his tongue thrust into his cheek and his elbows up, looking like a boy rather than a man in his late sixties.

The major persisted. "What's his problem? I saw your face when your grandmother said his name. You looked like you were going to pass out."

She turned to him and snapped, "He's been missing in action in Crete for two years, alright? So shut up about him."

She desperately wanted to talk to someone about Brian, but

Major Wilhelm was not the right person. She'd known Brian her whole life because their fathers were friends, and she had even gone out with him for a while when they were both in high school. But she'd lost contact with him until they met at a dance a few weeks before he was sent overseas; they'd been to a few movies together, eaten one dinner at a pub, and talked about what they would do when the war was over.

"I always thought we'd get married one day," he'd said.

She'd never thought that, but she'd smiled as if she had and changed the subject.

When he learned he was leaving to fight in Greece with the Second New Zealand Division, he'd asked her out for dinner, and they'd gone back to his flat for a drink. She was stupid. She knew that even at the time. But she was still caught off guard when he began begging her to stay the night because he might die without ever experiencing being with a woman. The night that followed was awful, at least for her, but he seemed pleased with himself. He talked about her as if she was now his for life, and it was hard to say anything honest as he was leaving to fight for his country. She hoped he would meet other women and forget about her.

And then he'd told his parents they were going to get married when he was home on leave, and everyone started to congratulate her on her engagement.

Now, he was missing, believed dead, and she felt obliged to stay loyal to him until she knew for certain what had happened to him, even though she was sure she would never marry him. Her father had told her he approved of her choice, and that didn't help.

She wanted to say to Wilhelm, 'I don't care about Brian; he feels like my brother, not a lover,' but of course she couldn't.

He'd think she wanted to dump a boyfriend who was overseas for one who was at hand because that's what so many women did.

Hamlet came back with the bike, his face flushed with pleasure.

"That was thrilling. Thanks for letting me have a ride. I've always wanted a motorcycle, but my wife is afraid I'll kill myself, and she'd be alone in this country."

"You're quite welcome," said Wilhelm. He mounted his bike. "Hop on the back, Kate. We'll take a spin around town, then I'll drop you off at the Roadster."

She climbed on behind him. There was barely room, and she found herself squashed against his back with nothing to hold on to except him.

"Are you in town for long?" asked Hamlet.

Wilhelm shrugged. "I have some work to do on the other side of the Manawatu Gorge. I'll be heading that way tomorrow."

"If you're near Pahiatua, come and see me. Kate knows where I live."

"I might take you up on that."

Hamlet waved at Granny, dozing on the hotel veranda, and asked, "What work is it you do, exactly?"

"I'm tracking down US Marines who've gone AWOL — absent without leave."

"Are there many of those? I thought the military camps were quite luxurious compared to what we have to put up with. Why would they want to run off?"

Wilhelm shrugged. "Lots of reasons. They've taken up with local women. Or they suddenly realize they're about to be shipped off to a war zone, and they don't want to die in battle."

"And you came up from Wellington today, did you?"

"I stopped off at Camp Russell. I ran into Kate there."

"My goodness, what were you doing at Camp Russell, Kate? Isn't that the American Marine camp?"

"I was on the way up to the farm — Max lent me his Roadster for the week — and saw Harry — Major Wilhelm drive into a ditch, so I stopped to help him."

"I see," said Hamlet. He stared at Wilhelm, his eyes narrowed slightly. "A major, eh? And they make you chase around the country looking for men who've gone absent without leave?"

Her uncle was more astute than she'd thought. He'd picked up on Wilhelm's rank, which she probably shouldn't have mentioned, now she thought about it.

She prodded Wilhelm's elbow. "Well, we'd better get going on our tour of Palmerston North. Are you taking Granny back to the farm, Uncle Ham? How will you get home?"

"One of the farm workers will bring me back to town, and I'll catch the train. I left my car at the station. I'll be home later today if you want to visit me there, Major Wilhelm."

"Thanks again, but I'm staying here tonight."

Hamlet glanced from Kate to Wilhelm. We're not an item, she wanted to say. We're just friends. Or something. She wasn't sure anymore. But if he kept calling her Kate, she was going to start calling him Harry. Harry. She liked the sound of that. And she liked the feel of his back against her chest as well. They fit together very nicely.

"Tell Granny I'll see her in a couple of hours," she said.

"I will," said Hamlet. "So you won't be coming to Pahiatua with Major Wilhelm?"

"Of course not," said Kate before the major could say anything. Hamlet was as bad as Granny at making her feel embarrassed.

"That's not a bad idea," said Wilhelm over his shoulder as they cruised around the Square. "You could drive, and we could check out all the small Scandinavian towns. What do you think? Might be fun."

"You'd have to come up with a better story than looking for deserters. Even Uncle Ham didn't go for that one."

"Does that mean you'll come with me?"

"No, it doesn't. I have a job, and I have to give my editor his car back."

"Well, if you insist. But it's an open invitation. Now, where should I go to find Scandinavians? Point the way."

They sped up the road to Bunnythorpe, scattering birds from the side of the road and throwing up gravel. In Bunnythorpe, she counted exactly three people on the streets: an old man with a cane, a woman with a basket over her arm heading off to shop at the grocery store, and a small boy pushing his sister in a pram.

She rested her chin on his shoulder. "Most of them will be in town for the funeral."

It had been a waste of time, but he didn't seem to mind, swerving around the single corner in town and crossing the train tracks.

"What about that factory over there? Is it in operation?"

"Glaxo? It's a dried milk factory. They make cereal for babies as well. You might find Germans working there, especially in the loading dock."

Hamlet's parents had lived in Bunnythorpe, and Hamlet had got his start at the Glaxo factory when it still belonged to the Nathans. He'd started as an occasional laborer and worked his way up to manager, buying shares in the company as it grew; he'd retired at sixty a wealthy man. He claimed to have invented the phrase, 'Glaxo Builds Bonnie Babies.' No one believed him, but they humored him when he made the claim.

There was no sign of her family in Bunnythorpe now other than in the cemetery. Granny's sister and her husband were buried there after suffering some horrible tragedies during the last war with their twin sons. Two of Hamlet's younger brothers and a sister were in different countries, making Granny and Kate his closest relatives in New Zealand.

"I'll check the factory."

He pulled up outside and strolled through the front door. She stayed astride the bike and watched him, admiring the confident way he walked into the factory. He came out a few minutes later.

"Closed for repairs. They had a fire in some outbuildings, and there's just an old security guard there. Let's take a ride around town and see if we can see anyone else."

A ride around Bunnythorpe did not take long, and eventually, he pulled up at the domain.

"What's that memorial over there? A war memorial?"

"Yes. From the Great War."

"New Zealand fought in World War I, then? Why? Europe's a long way from here."

"We think of ourselves as British. Some people still refer to England as Home, even if they were born here, so as soon as the war started, our government offered assistance. More than eighteen thousand men died fighting the Germans, and many more were injured. My Uncle Mikkel died at Gallipoli, and so did one of Hamlet's brothers."

He twisted around. "I'm sorry. I didn't mean to upset you with my stupid questions."

"I never knew Uncle Mikkle. But I sometimes think how awful

it must have been for Granny to lose a son like that. She got a letter from his colonel saying Uncle Mikkel didn't suffer, but I don't think it could be true."

"That's what the military always says. Why tell the mother or the wife the truth if they know it will make things worse?"

They rode back to Palmerston in silence, her forehead pressed against his leather jacket as she tried not to cry.

He helped her off at the spot where she had parked the Roadster and said,

"If you ever get a letter from the military saying I didn't suffer, don't believe them."

For a moment, she didn't know what to think. Why would she ever receive a letter from the military about his death? She changed the subject.

"Are you staying another night in town, as you told Uncle Ham?"

"Yeah. And at your grandmother's hotel, I guess."

"Goodbye then. I may see you around — if you keep following me."

"Same," he said, grinning. "I'm doing a tour of all the hotels tonight. I guess I won't see you downing a beer with the boys, will I?"

He roared off towards the Royal Hotel, and she watched him, partly to make sure he hadn't lied to her. She had very little doubt she would see him again. But if he intended to stay in Palmerston North and tour the bars, she had time to do what she'd been planning to do ever since he'd mentioned the men who had escaped from the internment camp. She would whip over to Pahiatua and find a story she could take back to Max, either about the fugitives, the conditions at the camp, or the injustice of putting citizens of German ancestry in prison. Max had spoken darkly about fifth columnists being among the refugees who had arrived just before the war, and she'd love to be able to prove him wrong. Besides that, she was curious about the man whose body she'd seen on the beach near Camp Russell. She might not be allowed to write about him, but she could find out for herself who he was.

She was in the Gorge in twenty minutes, racing around the curves, having a lovely time. The walls of the Gorge frequently slid onto the road, and she knew she was taking a chance going so fast, but she couldn't help herself. She felt as if it was in her blood to race through the Gorge.

She kept an eye on the mirror to see if he was following her but didn't see a motorcycle — just a man in a gray sedan who kept pulling up close to her car and falling back, no doubt wanting to make her pull over so he could pass. It was much too risky to pass her, even for a fool in a gray sedan.

Eventually, she gave in and pulled up on the grassy edge of the Gorge. At least it gave her a chance to look back at the road to make quite sure Harry wasn't somewhere behind her. The sedan cruised by, the driver staring straight ahead, and sped away. She climbed a rock and looked back. No sign of Harry Wilhelm. What a pity. She was half hoping to see him and his red motorcycle. Perhaps he was going on a pub crawl tonight, as unlikely as the story sounded.

She parked the car at the race track, surprised to see how different it looked. She'd come over here to the races many times, and the course had been easily accessed from anywhere on the road. Now, a tall chain link fence stopped anyone from getting in or out. She could see men wandering around inside the fence, chatting to each other and smoking. In one area, they were playing a game of bowls. The grandstand had been converted to what looked like a living area, the stairs and benches removed and replaced by a tin roof. Another high fence with barbed wire along the top had been built at one end of the grandstand where the bathrooms used to be. Four men sat on a bench inside, not talking, just staring straight ahead.

The problem she had now was how she would get inside. She'd assumed she could just stroll in, but clearly, that was not going to be possible. The guard on the gate looked serious. She considered flirting with him, but that was beneath her dignity. Instead, she strolled along the outer fence to see if she could see a friendly face.

She was almost to the edge of Hamlet's farm when she heard someone calling her.

"Miss Hardy, Miss Hardy…"

She stopped. A short, plump man wearing a baggy khaki outfit was hurrying towards her, waving to get her attention. The former steward of the Feilding race track, Dieter Schmidt.

"Mr. Schmidt, what are you doing in there? Aren't you a New Zealand citizen?"

He shrugged apologetically. "Well, I was born in Berlin, but I came here as a child. I never did apply for citizenship because I thought it didn't matter, and now I'm paying for it."

"That's terrible. How long have you been here?"

"A few weeks. I was on Somes Island for three months before that. I was called up and refused to go because I didn't want to fight my German cousins. I said I was a conscientious objector. They didn't approve, and the appeal board sent me here."

She clutched the wire and leaned towards him.

The guard at the gate yelled out. "Hey, madam, get away from the fence."

She backed away a few inches, unsure what to say to Mr. Schmidt. She suspected he was Jewish, but it would be rather insensitive to ask him if he was.

"Is it very boring in here?"

He nodded. "On Somes, they used to let us make paua shell ashtrays and bracelets, but then there were complaints that we were taking work away from disabled veterans. I've been thinking that I'd like to write down my story, but I haven't got any paper. I have a small pencil hidden in my mattress because they take anything sharp away from us, especially since the escape."

Kate tried not to look interested.

"I have an almost new notebook in my purse. I'll tell you what. I'll drop it through the fence. You can pick it up when I've gone."

She opened her purse and asked casually, "What escape, by the way? Did someone get out of here?"

"Four men," he said. "They captured two of them and put them in the special compound, but two are still missing. They put anyone with a criminal record in there as well. I'm glad they do. It's bad enough being Jewish in a camp full of Nazis without having to mix with criminals."

"You think there are Nazis in with you?" Kate asked, surprised.

He nodded. "I know there are. I hear what they say about me."

She looked along at the guard. He was eating a sandwich and not paying attention, so she pushed her new notebook through the fence and let it drop on the ground. "There. Don't get it yet. Wait until I've gone."

"Thank you so much, Miss Hardy. Were you looking for

someone in here? Can I get them for you?"

"I'm a reporter for the *Dominion*," she said. "I'm looking for a story. Do you have anything interesting to tell me about the escape?"

He rubbed his chin. "Well, right before the escape, there were some men here from the college — Massey College in Palmerston North. You must know it."

"Yes. Mostly agricultural courses, I think. I thought of doing a degree there, but they had nothing that interested me. I went to work in Wellington instead. What were they doing here, these men? Did you happen to catch a name?"

"I don't know why they were here, but they were talking to two of the men who escaped. I wouldn't be surprised if they helped. One of them was Professor ... now what was it? Collins? Something like that? Watch out, Miss Hardy, the guard..."

A hand grabbed her by the arm. "Alright, young lady. Time to go."

The guard had appeared behind her and was leering down at her as if he hadn't seen a woman for a while, which he probably hadn't. The camp was mostly men, as far as she could see. It seemed that women weren't capable of spying.

She pulled her arm away and marched off towards her car, remembering suddenly that she had written something in her notebook that she probably should have torn out. The name of the Marine Camp — Camp Russell. Well, nothing she could do about that now. And it wouldn't mean anything to Schmidt.

The guard followed her towards her car, so close that she could hear him breathing. Perhaps she should make a run for it just to see if he could keep up. Not likely. She'd been a champion sprinter all through school and had the ribbons to prove it.

"I'd leave her alone if I were you," shouted Schmidt. "You

don't know who her father is. You're taking your life in your hands."

Damn my father, Kate thought, *he always came up at the most inconvenient time.* She scuttled away and jumped into the Roadster.

She had intended to visit Hamlet. But she had an overwhelming urge to return to Palmerston North and ask questions at the college about the men who had visited the fugitives. It was probably for some harmless reason, but if they made her suspicious, it would give her something to lord it over the supercilious Harry Wilhelm.

But even as she thought of him, there he was, emerging from the edge of Hamlet's farm, looking secretive. She slammed on the brakes, angry now, and swerved off the road beside his bike.

7

Harry in Pahiatua

She had the kind of face that showed what she was thinking. Harry had known what she was planning almost as soon as she did; she was going to Pahiatua to talk to someone at the camp. Was she acting as a reporter, or was it something more? And why the hell had he told her not to believe it if she got a letter saying he'd died peacefully? He'd wanted to take it back as soon as it was out of his mouth. He sighed. He knew what he had to do, and that was to follow her to Pahiatua to see what she was up to. He just hoped if he ran into her there, she'd forgotten what he said, or at least paid no attention to it.

He sought out Benny the barman at the Royal Hotel and asked if there was a way to get to Pahiatua other than through the Manawatu Gorge. The last thing he wanted was for Kate to know he was following her.

"You could cross the ranges on the Pahiatua Track," said Benny. "Pretty windy, though. I saw you had a bike. You could easily get blown off the road."

"Let me worry about that. Just tell me how to get there. Show me on this map."

"Out this road here," said Benny, running his finger along a blue line that ran towards the ranges. "Go past Massey College and turn left here. Then, in about five minutes — less than that for you — turn right. There should be a sign on the corner saying it's the Pahiatua Track. From there, the road just goes up and up until it goes down. One big hill."

Harry folded the map and stuck it in his pocket. "Thank you, Benny. Much appreciated."

Benny gave him a sly look. "You're a Yank, aren't you? Don't forget to drive on the left. The road's steep with lots of curves, and sometimes you'll run into logging trucks coming the other way. Plus, the wind is terrible, and it's hard to control a car, let alone a bike. You could come around a corner and be over a cliff or on the bonnet of a truck before you know it."

Harry grinned at him. "So, stay on the left, and don't get blown off a cliff by the wind. Got it."

Benny picked up a rag and started polishing a glass, not looking at Harry. After a minute, he glanced up and asked, "Are you and Kate...?"

"Absolutely not," said Harry, more definitely than he felt.

As Benny had warned, the Pahiatua track was steep. It reminded Harry of the Pacific Coast Highway in California, with a forest instead of an ocean on the side. It started as a normal hill with a winding road, but as he neared the top, it got steeper and steeper, swinging wildly around bends with high banks on one side and waves of deep, treed ravines on the other. Once he passed the crest and headed down towards Pahiatua, things did not improve. Several times, he cruised around a curve with fields on either side and discovered that the road in front of him had dropped away abruptly. Great scenery, but he preferred not to become part of it. He gritted his teeth, tightened his grip on the handlebars, made sure he kept on the left side of the road, and eventually, he was down on the plains below, still in one piece.

From the ranges, the road to Pahiatua meandered between farmland and rivers until he arrived at what could only be the main street, a broad boulevard with a grassy strip the width of a football field running down the center. He cruised up beside a boy of about ten trying to mount a woman's bicycle three sizes too large for him and asked where Mr. Sorensen's farm was, adding that he'd heard it was near the old race track.

"That way," said the boy, almost dropping the bicycle as he let go of the handlebars to point south. "But it's not a race track anymore. They built a prison for German spies and conchies on it."

"Really? I didn't know that. And where's the Sorensen farm relative to this prison?"

"Just past the prison on the same side. You'll see the gate with his name on it. You can't miss it."

"Well, thank you for your help, son. Much obliged."

The boy looked at him up and down. "Are you a Yank soldier?"

"A Yank," agreed Harry. "But not a soldier. Soldiers are in the army. I'm a Marine."

"I thought they were the same thing. In my comic books, it just says soldiers. How many Japs have you killed?"

Harry pretended to think about it. "Hmm. Maybe fifty ... or is it sixty. Not sure, but plenty."

The boy's jaw dropped.

"Jeepers! I'm going to tell my friends about you. A Marine who's killed that many Japs? I bet you're one of their top blokes. They should make a comic book about you."

He wobbled away, intent on reporting his new information to the first person who crossed his path.

Harry took off down the road out of town going south, keeping his eye open for the race track and for Kate.

He spotted her as he passed what had once been a race track, a fenced area converted to a camp — for German spies and conchies, as the kid had informed him. She was leaning against the chain link fence talking to a thickset man with dark curly hair, wearing the khaki uniform with the red star that indicated he was in the custody of the state. The Roadster was parked on the grassy area nearby. He slowed down to minimize the noise his bike made and glided past her just as she glanced towards the guard on the gate and shoved something small through the fence. The object dropped to the ground, but the man made no effort to pick it up, pretending he hadn't seen her drop it. What the hell was it? Not paper as it had dropped like a stone. A book of some kind, he thought, but something she didn't want the guard to see. And who was he, the man she was meeting? A German, of course, if he was in the internment camp. What did that make her? Was she more loyal to Germany than she seemed?

Damn. He'd been hoping she wasn't involved in all this, but it looked increasingly like she could be. And on top of the way she acted, why was she untouchable? Why had the officer at the S.I.B. told him to stay away from her? Was she a known spy? Would he be interfering with an ongoing surveillance if he confronted her with what he had seen?

He found Hamlet's horse farm a few minutes down the road. The gate was open, the entrance guarded by a cattle grid, although no animals were to be seen. A road between a line of poplar trees ran up to a large bungalow. He rode up towards the house and pulled up near the door. As he dismounted from his bike, Hamlet emerged from the front door, smiling broadly, his hands out to Harry.

"Major Wilhelm. What a nice surprise. I thought you were spending another night in Palmerston?"

"My boss telegraphed me about a missing marine hiding out down in Masterton. I was on my way there to check the story, and I saw your name on the gate. I knew you lived around here somewhere, so I came up to check."

"Well, I'm glad you did. Come and have a snifter with me. I hate to drink alone, and my wife believes in abstaining from anything enjoyable."

Harry guessed a snifter must be some kind of alcohol. "Sure."

"I'll have Helga bring us our drinks in my study."

Harry followed Hamlet into a book-lined room that was Hamlet's study, although there was no sign he used it for actual work. No desk, but two large leather chairs sat on either side of an ornately carved wooden table covered with framed photographs of Hamlet with various dignitaries, including Prime Minister Peter Fraser. A mahogany box beside the photographs looked like an old gun box, the type used to store the type of pistols one would use for a dual and not much use for practical purposes. He was itching to check inside but decided it wouldn't be polite.

As if by magic, an older woman appeared carrying a tray with two brandy glasses and a fancy crystal decanter filled with a dark liquid and placed it beside Harry.

He gestured at the tray. "My grandfather owned a decanter just like that."

"Bohemian crystal," said Hamlet. "I bought it in Bohemia when I met my wife. I was touring Europe after the first war —

I was looking for racing stock for my farm — riding horses that were used by officers. Helga's father was an officer, and she was selling his horses. Horses were a bargain after the war. Helga is Bohemian, you know, from what is now called Sudetenland. Helga, this is Kate's friend, Major Wilhelm."

Helga stared at her husband expressionlessly and then bobbed her head at Harry. She was all gray: gray hair, gray dress, and pale skin free of makeup.

"Sudetenland? That's part of Germany now, isn't it? Was it part of Czechoslovakia when you were there?" Harry hoped he didn't sound rude. The Nazis had been given the German-speaking part of Czechoslovakia with the Munich Agreement long after Helga had left, but the German speakers had wanted their land returned to Germany even before the war.

"It was," said Hamlet, glancing at his wife. "Helga, have you taken Jens his tea?"

Helga nodded abruptly. She didn't seem to have much to say for herself. She'd probably been beaten down by her experiences in the past few years, especially if she'd retained her accent. Kate had said that Germans or anyone who sounded German had been harassed by the locals since the start of the war.

The windows of the study looked out at the back of the property. He was sipping his brandy and chatting to Hamlet about cars and motorcycles when he saw Helga emerge from the kitchen. She was clutching a tray with a tea towel draped over it — taking food to someone, he guessed. He could see a small wooden hut in the distance, and as she approached it, the door opened, and a man wearing khaki clothing and a large floppy hat that concealed his face stepped through the door and watched her walk towards him. He was thin and hunched over.

He looked elderly.

Harry finished his drink and rose to his feet.

"Well, I must be on my way. Got a bit of a ride today."

As he exchanged parting pleasantries with Hamlet, he saw her place the tray on the ground and turn back towards the house. Once she was out of sight, the man picked up the food and disappeared around the back of the hut. This must be the Jens that Hamlet had mentioned.

His senses on high alert, he drove down the tree-lined track and leaned his bike against the fence at the edge of the property. He jumped the fence and made his way around the fence to the hut. He could see Hamlet, still sitting in his library with a full glass of brandy, his back to the window. Keeping out of sight as best he could, he peered through the tiny window of the hut. An old-fashioned kerosene lamp flickered on a table beside a chair. But he could see no one in there until a movement alerted him. A shape had moved into the frame, blocking the light from the lamp.

With a jolt, he realized that he was staring into the faded blue eyes of an elderly man. It was hard to tell how old he was, but close to Hamlet's age. And although he was staring in Harry's direction, he seemed not to see him. Harry had seen the look before. Someone had called it the thousand-yard stare, the look of someone who had seen more fighting than any human could handle. He believed in the First World War, they'd called it shell shock.

Who was he then? The hut looked comfortable, with a chair and a bed. A radio sat on the table beside the lamp. The man turned away from the window and picked up a packet of cigarettes from the table. He pulled one out with shaking fingers. He was a survivor of the last war, that was clear. But which side had he fought on? And why was he hidden out here? Did Hamlet know about him? Did Kate? He remembered that Hamlet had asked Helga if she had fed Jens yet. This man must be Jens. Therefore, Hamlet must know he was here.

One thing he was sure of. From his appearance, he was either Scandinavian or German.

And not one of the men who had escaped from the camp, or probably not. Too old.

He opened the door and stepped in softly, trying not to scare the poor old man.

"Hello, Jens. How are you feeling today."

Jens dropped into the chair, put his arm over his head, and moaned loudly.

Harry squatted beside him and took his hand, in the process knocking over a small pile of shells. Jens reached down and scrabbled at the shells.

"Ruined," he said. "Ruined."

"Sorry, Jens. Here, let me help you get them piled up again."

Jens sat back and watched as Harry picked up the shells and balanced them awkwardly on his table.

"Where's Paul?" he asked suddenly. "Is he coming home soon?"

Paul must be a relative who'd been killed in the war, but Harry didn't want to stir up memories.

"Helga will be out to see you soon," he said, playing it safe.

"I don't like Helga," said Jens. "She wanted to call in the Mental Defectives Board to look at me. I'm alright. I just get muddled sometimes."

He bent his head away from Harry and began tidying up the shells, sorting them into three piles of different shades.

"And Paul wouldn't like her either."

He stopped sorting his shells, looked Harry in the eye with a half smile on his lips, and added, "Paul was at Sari Bair, you know. The Turks were as bad as the Germans."

Harry nodded as if he had a clue where Sari Bair was. Turkey, he guessed. "So I heard. Well, I must be off. It was nice talking with you, Jens."

"Please come again," said Jens, his voice formal, sounding as if they had just had a cup of tea together. "Did you come over the fence with the other men? They've gone now, but you could catch up to them if you hurry."

"What fence?" asked Harry. Had Jens seen something?

"The race track fence, of course. There was a fire, and fire engines, and shouting, and some men came over the fence. I was worried it was the war again, but Helga told me not to worry, they were on our side."

He could see Jens' hand starting to tremble. Time to leave. He'd seen the men escaping, apparently, and Helga had calmed him down. Good for her. Or did she mean they were on the same side?

He backed out of the hut slowly, smiling at Jens the whole time. Poor bastard. His war had ended twenty-five years earlier. Had he been like this ever since? For a minute, he imagined himself as an old man, sitting in a hut behind someone's house, being brought his meals. And, very briefly, he imagined that it was a still-young Kate who was bringing him his meals. He shook his head. What the hell was going on with him that she kept appearing in his head? He wasn't ready to get involved with a woman in this country. Especially not one with odd connections like hers.

He retraced his steps to his bike, and, as if she had materialized from his thoughts, she pulled up in the Roadster and jumped out.

"Are you spying on my uncle? And what are you doing in Pahiatua? I thought you were going to do a round of the pubs in Palmerston tonight."

The only way he could argue with her was to attack.

"Why is your uncle keeping a prisoner in a hut behind his house?"

"He's not a prisoner. He can leave whenever he wants. But he isn't well. He was in the war…"

"On which side?"

"What do you mean? Our side, of course. He was at Gallipoli. His twin brother Paul was killed, and Jens survived, but he came home in a terrible state — shell shock."

"Why keep him in a hut? Why not in the house?"

"He wants to be alone, that's why. He was fine until the war started. He worked in the lumberyard and was happy enough, but then people began saying terrible things to him because they thought he was German. It was too much after all he'd been through, so Hamlet let him use the hut out the back."

She was telling the truth, that was obvious. But he still had questions he wanted to ask about Helga and Hamlet. She'd be upset if he asked about her relatives, so he asked the question that was bothering him the most.

"What were you doing at the camp?"

"You were following me, weren't you? How come I didn't see you behind me."

"I came over the Pahiatua Track."

She stared at him, her brows lowered, her lips tightly pinched, her cheeks dark pink.

"Well, it's none of your bloody business what I was doing at the camp. They caught two of the men, by the way. One is still at large."

"I could have found that out myself, but thanks anyway. I hope you haven't got any more snooping in mind. There's a murderer on the loose, and if you keep on messing with my operation, you'll get yourself killed."

"That would be very convenient for you, wouldn't it?"

He shook his head and sighed. Women, why did they always make such ridiculous arguments?

"Look, do what you damn well like, but I'm going to stand here until I see you heading down the road to the Gorge on your way back to Palmerston North."

She spun around and stormed off to the car, pulling away in a swirl of dust and gravel that kicked up into his face. He watched her until she was out of sight. His plans had changed. If she had anywhere else to go, he needed to know why and where.

Whatever she said, he needed to follow her.

8

Massey College

She didn't think he was following her as she made a hard turn onto the grounds of Massey College. She'd stopped the car several times, parked on the side of the road against the hill, and waited to see if he would shoot by, but he hadn't. How disappointing.

Massey College had changed since the last time she'd been here when she'd attended a dance given by the Ag students, a bunch of burly, rugby-playing farm boys; they were all learning how to swing and do the jitterbug. She had been quite dizzy by the end of the evening. It had been fun, however, even though many of the boys were about to be shipped overseas.

Back then, early in the war, the College still specialized in agriculture, but within two years, the student body was down to fewer than four dozen students. Then, in 1941, an Army Staff Training College had been established, and the place was once more busy with activity — military activity as well as farming activity as Massey continued to fulfill its original purpose. Apart from dehydrating butter, including that from Granny's farm, the College was experimenting with new breeds of cows and chickens and new strains of wheat and corn. There was a feeling in the air that when the war finished, they would be ready to move forward.

She drove onto the grounds of the College and along the short track to the Oval, now with prefabricated huts for the officer-trainees in the center. The main building, a somewhat imposing structure that the original planners had envisioned as an Antipodean Oxford or Cambridge, was on the far side of the oval. The foundations of a new building were evident near the gate — an Army Staff Officers' Hostel, she had heard.

The College had also begun developing courses to train returning servicemen. She couldn't help thinking that it was disconcerting that everyone was preparing for 'When the war is over' when they had no idea if it would ever end.

She parked the roadster outside the main building and went inside. A woman in her thirties, her hair pulled back tightly, her eyebrows drawn in a thin line, sat behind a desk filing her nails, which were painted bright red to match the shade of her lipstick. Kate couldn't help wondering where she'd found enough coupons to pay for her makeup.

She smiled at her as warmly as she could at the woman.

"Good afternoon. Professor Collins wouldn't happen to be in, would he?"

The woman shrugged and kept on with her nails.

"Could you ring his office?

She sighed loudly and picked up a telephone from her desk with her fingertips.

"Whom shall I say is asking for him?"

"Kate Hardy, from *The Dominion*. I want to talk to him about the new program for retraining returning soldiers."

The woman slammed the receiver back on its cradle and

frowned at Kate.

"Professor Collins? Are you sure you have the right name? He's not involved in the training programs. He's a researcher. Colonel Hawkins is in charge of the retraining program."

Kate improvised quickly. "I wanted to interview professors who've been here for a while. See if they have any concerns about the influx of officer trainees, if there are enough facilities, that sort of thing."

The woman shook her head. "He knows absolutely nothing about the retraining programs and even less about the officer trainees. He arrived quite recently. I'm sorry, but he won't be able to help you."

"If you're looking for Professor Collins, I just saw him outside," said a voice from behind her.

Kate turned. A young man in an officer's uniform, his hat tucked under his arm, smiled at her.

"Whereabouts was he?"

"Out by the special mating pens." The officer trainee gave a wry grin. "He's wringing the necks of chickens. It's not a pleasant sight, but I assume it needs to be done. If you turn left out of the door and go around behind the building, you'll see the pens. He's with a couple of his Animal Science students. Have your smelling salts ready."

Kate managed not to let her jaw drop at the thought of a professor wringing chickens' necks. What was Professor Collins up to? How on earth did wringing chickens' necks relate to research? She thanked the young officer trainee and went in search of the professor. Behind her, she heard the receptionist berating the trainee.

"Why on earth did you tell her that? She'll write about it for her newspaper, and everyone will think Professor Collins is some kind of fiend."

She heard the chickens shrieking as she rounded the corner of the building and immediately came upon the mating pens, which looked exactly like chicken coops. An older man and a pair of boys too young for the armed forces were wringing chickens' necks and tossing the corpses into a large crate. The scene of carnage left her gagging for a moment.

She stood and waited to be noticed, and eventually, the older man, who was wearing a bloody butcher's apron and voluminous gumboots, stopped what he was doing and came towards her, frowning and wiping his hands on the apron.

"Are you looking for someone, ma'am?"

She nodded, making an effort to smile.

"Professor Collins?"

"Yes. I'm Professor Collins. Who might you be?"

"Kate Hardy from *The Dominion*. I wanted to speak with someone who taught here but not with the Officers Training School. I'm working on an article about the research being done by the College, and the woman at the desk sent me around to speak with you. I didn't realize you'd be so busy."

"Lina sent you? Well then, I suppose I could take a few minutes to answer some questions," he said, looking a little more friendly. "Could you wait until we finish with these hens? We'll be done in ten minutes."

"Alright," she said, trying not to look at the two young men who seemed to be enjoying their task a little too much, tossing the chicken corpses into the crate as if they were throwing rugby balls. "My car's parked in front of the main building. I'll wait for you there."

She sat in her car thinking about how she could bring up his visit to the internment camp without making him suspicious.

He didn't look particularly Germanic, and he had an English name and no trace of an accent. He'd probably been at the camp for something to do with his research, but it was odd that he'd spoken with the men who'd escaped.

He arrived eventually and slipped into the passenger seat, patting the leather on the seat appreciatively as he sat down.

"How does a young woman like you come to be driving such an expensive car? You're not one of the Feilding Hardys, are you?"

Kate had been asked before if she was one of the Feilding Hardys, and she was, although she preferred that no one knew.

"We're distantly related, I think," she said.

"Then you must also be related to Sam Hardy."

She looked him straight in the eye, hoping her father would understand, and said, "Not that I know of. Is he also one of the Feilding crowd?"

He made a humphing sound and shrugged. "So, what was it you wanted to discuss?"

She had decided to begin with the chickens.

"I heard you've been working on a new breed..."

"Of chickens?" he asked, his eyes lighting up. "Is that out already? I was hoping to beat the Canterbury Agricultural College to the punch. We're always competing with each other."

She nodded. "Yes, some of it's out, anyway. But I just saw you destroying them. What went wrong?"

"White Eye," he said. "We were breeding the White Leghorn, trying to increase egg production, but we've discovered they're prone to White Eye, which reduces egg production from the hens instead of increasing it, which is not useful in the present situation. We're getting rid of them and starting again. The poultry farmers rely on us to send them the best breeders."

"Couldn't you give the healthy ones to someone? It seems rather harsh to kill them."

He gave her an angry look. "I suppose it might seem that way, but our mandate is to develop the best animal we can. We can't have hens out there carrying the Massey College imprimatur that are sickly and able to lay only a few eggs. It would undercut our credibility. I'm sure you have no experience with this kind of thing, Miss Hardy."

"My grandfather bred horses," she said. "I never heard of him killing any because they didn't perform well enough."

"Now, that's simply not true," he said. "You must know that when a horse breaks a leg, it has to be destroyed. I'm sure your grandfather would tell you that."

She was about to agree with him, as she had once seen Uncle Hamlet put a horse down at the Pahiatua Race Track when it fell and broke its leg, but he carried on speaking before she had a chance.

"It's the same with humans," he said. "You simply can't breed a good specimen with an inferior one and expect a good result; sometimes, all one can do is eliminate the weak ones. Take the Māori, for example..."

She sat back in her seat, shocked.

"What?"

Who did he bloody well think he was, saying things like that?

"I have to go," she said abruptly. "Could you get out of my car, please?"

He looked down his nose at her for a minute, then climbed from the car and slammed the door. As she sped off, she remembered she had wanted to ask him about why he was at the internment camp, but she didn't care anymore. He probably wanted to use the Germans there as breeding stock. He was a bloody Nazi, that's what he was.

She raced through the gate and onto the road into town without stopping and almost collided with a Jeep. Dark sunglasses hid the driver's face, and for a minute, she thought it was Harry. She barely avoided swerving off the road, craning her neck around to look back to see if it was him, and saw him staring back.

But if it was Harry, he'd changed his clothes and his vehicle in the last hour. A Jeep instead of a bike, and a dark blue pullover instead of a leather jacket. Not Harry, then. Maybe another American because of the Jeep and because the Americans all looked so darn healthy. She waved a quick apology and headed back towards the farm, feeling disappointed.

She'd calmed down by the time she reached the farm. Betty was in the paddock turning over what she called her Victory Garden, kneeling in the dirt with a trowel, singing a Vera Lynn song at the top of her lungs, making it sound somewhat like a dirge. "I'll be seeing you in all the old, familiar places..."

Kate pulled up the car beside the cottage and got out.

"What a lovely voice you have, Betty."

Betty spun around. "Miss Hardy. I didn't hear you come in. I was singing loudly because I thought no one was around to overhear. Have you just arrived?"

"I arrived last night. I didn't want to knock on your door as it looked like you and Tom were about to go to bed."

Betty avoided Kate's eyes, blushing. "We did go to bed rather early last night. It's our anniversary today. Tom has gone into Feilding to see if he can buy something special for our tea. We've been hoarding our coupons for a nice piece of roast beef."

"I wish I'd known. I have plenty of coupons. I could have

given you some."

Betty took off the scarf that had been wrapped around her head and shook out her hair. Kate noticed, not for the first time, how pretty she was. What was she doing married to an older man with a limp? Surely she could have had anyone she wanted? They'd left England before the war started and before all the men went off to fight in Europe and North Africa. She must have had plenty of men to pick from — not that Tom wasn't a lovely man and very much in love with his wife.

"I was hoping to take Southern Cross out for a gallop," she said. "Have you ridden her today?"

Betty smiled. "Just a short ride. I was going to take her out again as soon as I finished turning over the garden. She needs a good run."

Kate was torn. She had been dying to take her horse for a long gallop over the fields, but she knew Betty loved riding Southern Cross, and it didn't seem fair to swan in and take her pleasure away from her, especially on her anniversary.

"I had some rather bad news yesterday," Betty added. "I've been trying to keep busy, so I don't think about it."

Kate moved over beside her and put her arm around her shoulder. "Can you tell me, or would you rather not?"

Betty's eyelids fluttered. "I have to tell someone. I couldn't tell Tom because he was so happy, and he's been so down lately." She wiped away an unseen tear with the back of her hand. "My brother has been captured by the Germans. He was in North Africa with a tank division and was captured by Rommel's troops. I don't know where they'll take him or where he is now. I'm terrified about what they might do to him."

Kate thought about Brian, who was either a captive or dead. At least Betty knew her brother was alive. Not knowing was much harder. But she could hardly say that to Betty.

"The Germans will take care of him," she said, not believing it herself. "They're not monsters, and there's the Geneva Convention..."

Betty's back stiffened. "But they are monsters," she said, frowning at Kate. "Haven't you heard what they're doing to Jewish people? The mass shootings in Poland, the camps where they torture and kill anyone they think of as vermin. Perhaps you don't know this, Miss Hardy, but Tom and I are Jewish, which is why we came to New Zealand, as far away from the Nazis as we could get. We were very lucky to be British citizens, or else they would never have accepted us. They didn't ask us our religion, fortunately."

And, of course, her brother must also be Jewish, but would that matter if he was a prisoner of war? Kate didn't know, but she pitied Betty.

"Betty, why don't you take Southern Cross out for a ride? I have to talk to Granny anyway, and it's going to be dark soon."

Betty gave a deep sigh. "That would be lovely, thank you, Miss Hardy..."

"And could you please stop calling me Miss Hardy? My name is Kate."

"Thank you, Kate. I wish it wasn't so cold, though. I've been meaning to get myself a riding jacket as soon as I've saved up enough coupons. It's always about the coupons, isn't it?"

Kate stripped off her jacket. "Here, take mine for now. I'll pop down and fetch it in the morning."

Betty shrugged on the coat, which was a little large for her, and went into the stable. Kate wanted to go with her, but now she was cold herself, so she jumped back into the car and drove up to the main house. Southern Cross could wait for another day.

Granny was standing at the front door waiting for her, a shawl around her shoulders.

"I heard the car coming," she said. "What are you doing without a coat? You must be freezing. Come inside; I have a fire going."

"I lent my jacket to Betty," said Kate. "She told me a sad story about her brother and I ... what was that?"

Granny hurried down the steps and stood beside Kate, staring in the direction of the sound. "That was a gunshot. It came from over there, along the ridge."

"Could it be a hunter? It isn't deer season, is it?"

"Rabbits, perhaps," said Granny. "Or a wild pig. But it's on our land, and I haven't given anyone permission to shoot anything."

Kate felt goose bumps rising on the back of her neck, and she knew it wasn't from the cold. Could it be something to do with Betty and Tom? There were some terrible people in the district; she knew that because of the way they treated Scandinavians.

"I'll go down and make sure Betty and Southern Cross are alright. Go inside, Granny, and lock the door. Telephone the police and tell them it's urgent. They'll come out here for you right away."

"If you think it's necessary. I'll tell them it's Sam Hardy's farm, and they'll be here before I hang up the telephone. Be careful, darling. I'm sure it's nothing, but you never know with all the awful things that are happening to our friends lately."

Kate sprinted down the hill to the cottage. Perhaps it was just a boy out shooting rabbits, not realizing he needed permission from the landowner, but Kate knew the sound of different guns, and that was not a rabbit gun she'd just heard. Someone had fired a round from a rifle. One single shot that had echoed along the ridge. Anyone who limited themselves to a single shot must have thought they'd hit whatever it was they were shooting at. And she was terrified that either Betty or Southern Cross had been the target.

9

The Gunshot

Harry Wilhelm watched Kate driving away towards the entrance to the Gorge, punched himself on the thigh, and cursed loudly. He didn't have time for this stupidity. He had a killer to catch. On the other hand, he wanted to know something, anything, about her family. Something was not right with her family. It may not relate to his case, but he couldn't be sure. And if it was related to the case and he let her go, he'd be pissed off at himself.

He gave her a twenty-minute start and then took off through the Gorge. The thought of driving back over the Pahiatua Track gave him the creeps, even though he'd once driven his bike off a ten-foot cliff — on purpose — when he was chasing someone. The locals must have nerves of steel to drive on roads like that. Did they just accept the fact that if they went into a ditch, it would be a thousand feet deep and would kill them?

The Gorge road was better, twisting and turning along a raging river with steep hills on either side, but he was riding in the left lane against the hill, and it was easier not to lose his focus. He ignored the signs that warned of slips after rain and concentrated on not getting killed by an oncoming motorist.

At the other side of the Gorge, the road split in two, one side curving past Massey College and into Palmerston North, the other to Bunnythorpe, and then on to Feilding. He couldn't see any sign of Kate to the left unless she'd dodged into the College to lose him, so he turned right and headed towards her family farm. She'd better damn well tell him what the hell was going on, who her father was, and why he'd been told to stay away from her. The situation was messing with his mission, and he needed it cleared away.

He knew roughly where the farm was. His map showed a road running past the farm gate, parallel to a ridge that divided the property that would take him right to the gate.

It took him almost an hour to get there, and the sun was setting as he approached the house. He still wasn't used to winter in the middle of June but imagined that Christmas would be even weirder when Santa Claus probably arrived dressed in khaki shorts and rubber-soled sandals with Bing Crosby crooning *White Christmas* in the background.

He was unreasonably happy when he saw her coming through the gate on her horse, her hair flying out behind her. She's leading you along, an inner voice said. Down boy.

He pulled over and waited for her to reach him, seated astride his bike, his arms crossed, grinning to himself.

When she suddenly rose above the horse and seemed to suspend herself there, he was surprised but not worried. She was showing off for him.

Then, the sound of the shot echoed past him.

She was falling, spinning off towards the ground without trying to halt her fall. She hit the grass at the edge of the road and rolled over several times. And he knew for sure that she'd

THE GUNSHOT

been shot.

He hurled his bike into the ditch and sprinted towards her, yelling her name, desperate to find her alive. In the back of his mind, his fighting brain kept spinning, trying to work out where the shot had come from and whether she was still in danger. From up on the ridge, he thought. The ridge that ran between the upper and lower fields of the farm.

He reached her and slid down beside the prone figure, lying on her side with her arms flung upwards and her hair covering her face. He could see blood seeping through her jacket just below her shoulder. Hadn't hit an artery, thank God, and she wasn't dead. But it had been close.

He pushed her hair back and bent forward, staring at her, puzzled. What had happened? Who was this in his arms?

Then someone yelled his name.

Kate had emerged through the farm gate and was sprinting towards him, no longer wearing the blood-covered jacket now worn by the woman on the ground.

"Harry, Harry, what happened? We heard a shot..."

He rolled the injured woman onto her back and saw her eyelids flutter.

"She's not dead. She took a shot in the shoulder, and it knocked her off the horse."

Kate knelt beside him and took the woman's hand in hers. "My horse, Harry, and my jacket. Someone thought they were shooting at me, and they've hurt poor Betty. If she's hurt badly, I'll never forgive myself."

He raised Betty to a seated position and gently started to remove the jacket. Her eyes shot open, and she gasped when he tried to pull her injured arm from the sleeve so he could check the wound. He undid the buckle on the side of his boot and pulled his fighting knife from its sheath.

"Hold her still; I'm going to cut off the sleeve of the jacket."

Kate positioned herself behind Betty and laid Betty's elbow across her knee.

"Try not to move, Betty," she said. "Major Wilhelm knows what he's doing. He's going to cut off the sleeve and make sure you aren't bleeding too much. Granny's calling the police, and they'll get an ambulance here very quickly."

Betty moaned. "Tom..."

Kate glanced at Wilhelm. "Tom's her husband." She patted Betty's hand. "Betty, we'll make sure Tom follows you into Feilding as soon as he gets home."

Wilhelm pulled the sleeve away slowly.

"The shot came from the ridge," he said quietly. "We're shielded by the hedge down here, but keep low. Did you see anything?"

"No, but Granny and I heard the shot, and we both thought it came from the ridge."

"Good. And just the one, so he must think he had a hit. Listen, Betty, it looks like the bullet went into your shoulder under your armpit. I'm sure it hurts like hell, but you're going to be fine."

She gave him a weak smile. "Thank you, sir."

Kate raised Betty slightly. "There's no blood on her back. Are you sure it went right through?"

He leaned over to examine her back. "Nope. It's still in there. How long before an ambulance arrives and takes her to the hospital? Give me your worst-case scenario."

"It's at least an hour for them to get here and take her back to Feilding. Palmerston would be better, but it would take even longer. There's a proper surgeon at the Palmerston hospital. He's a bit old, but he knows what he's doing."

"Betty, do you have any kind of alcohol in your cottage I can use to clean the wound?"

Betty smiled. "We don't drink, but Tom has a first aid kit an army friend gave him. There's some Sulfonamide powder..."

"Thank Christ for that," said Harry. "Kate, I'm going to carry her into the cottage and get the bullet out. Go ahead and make sure all the doors are open so we can go right in. And find the first aid kit and anything I can use to clean my knife. Betty, you're very brave, and I'm going to make sure you stay strong and healthy."

Kate vaulted onto her horse and trotted back towards the gate, bent low and staying in the shelter of the hedge. He picked up Betty and saw her eyes roll back in her head as she passed out from the pain. While she was still out, he strode towards the gate with her in his arms, trying not to jolt her shoulder.

Kate had stabled her horse and was waiting for them at the door. She slammed it shut after them.

"I found the first aid kit. There's some of that powder in it. What can I do to help?"

"Boil water. And find something to clean my knife."

He carried Betty into the only bedroom of the cottage, noticing as he did an old rifle in a glass case on the wall at the end of the bed. An odd place to keep a rifle, but maybe Tom was a collector.

Kate dropped the first aid kit on the bed and went in search of something to clean his knife. She returned with a bottle of clear liquid.

"Will this do the trick? It's an antiseptic for cleaning sinks, and it has carbolic acid in it. I found a bag of cotton wool as well, so you can pack the wound and a roll of Elastoplast."

He felt a momentary surge of annoyance at the difference in

language. They would communicate much better if the locals just used American words and brand names.

"Open the lid and lower the knife blade into it. Then pour half of it on my hands."

When she'd finished, he picked up the knife and knelt on the floor. Betty was watching him apprehensively.

"I'm sorry, Betty, but this will hurt. Can you be brave while I get the bullet out?"

"Can I bite down on a belt?" she asked. "I saw that in a film once."

"A swig of whiskey would be better," he said, smiling at her. "But you can have my belt to bite on if you think it will help. Kate, will you do the honors?"

She lifted his jacket and undid the belt buckle.

"Will it come out if I give it a pull?"

"Of course."

She drew the belt slowly from around his waist.

"Here, Betty. I'll put it between your teeth."

She opened her mouth to take the belt, distracted for a moment, and he put his fingers on either side of the entry wound and pulled it apart. Her jaws clamped down on the leather, and she made a muffled groan.

He inserted the knife into the wound and moved it gently. He felt the bullet right away, nestled in the flesh of her armpit. It hadn't gone into a bone, and he didn't think it had clipped a tendon or an artery either. He moved the tip of the blade and began to pry out the bullet.

"Here it comes," he said as confidently as he could. If he'd been a praying man, he would have been asking God for help because he knew he wasn't close to being an expert. He'd done this in battle a couple of times, but not to a young woman who had known nothing about war. The bullet lifted into view, and he eased it out gently with his fingers. Betty was writhing in pain, with Kate pressing down on her shoulders.

"There. Got it."

He dropped shell on the bed.

"Hand me that cotton stuff and then those elastic things."

He saw a smile flit over Kate's face as she complied.

"There. You can stop chomping on my belt now, Betty. I'll help you sit up."

He put his arm across her back and lifted her forward; she spat out the belt and started to retch. Kate rubbed her back and made soothing sounds.

The front door of the cottage creaked open, and they both sat up.

"Katie, are you in here?"

"We're in the bedroom, Granny."

"Oh my goodness, what happened? I was worried. I rang the police and told them to come up from the Feilding road and over the hill. They should be here any minute."

"Good work, Granny," said Harry. "That way, they'll come in facing the exit and won't have to turn around. But you took a chance, coming down here. He's probably still out there." And you walked right past him, he thought. But he hadn't shot at her, so that meant something. She wasn't the one he was after. He knew that already.

"How do you know it's a man?" she asked. "Frank tangled with a female sharpshooter once. Sort of like Annie Oakley, she was. But one of her accomplices killed her before he could."

He raised one eyebrow at Kate, and she gave a small shrug. She'd heard all sorts of fantastical stories in her life, he was sure. Mrs. Hardy was remembering a book she'd read or a movie she'd seen. But Mrs. Hardy had made a good point. A female sharpshooter was less likely, but he shouldn't rule it out.

"Did you hear anyone up on the ridge, Mrs. Hardy?"

"It was very quiet," she said. "Too quiet, I think. I could feel him watching me, but I knew I wasn't the one he wanted to shoot, so I felt safe. Why did he shoot at Betty, Katie? Was it because she was riding your horse and wearing your coat?"

Harry gave a short nod and moved Betty back a few inches. She looked as if she was fading, and he didn't want her to fall asleep. "Any idea when the police will be here?"

"I can hear a siren in the distance," said Kate. "Listen. It's very faint, but it's coming this way."

Harry heard it as well.

"Find a blanket for Betty," he said. "We can't wait for an ambulance. We'll have the police take her to the hospital. To Palmerston if they can."

Tom arrived just as Harry was carrying Betty out to a police car driven by a single constable from the Feilding station. He'd arrived in the oldest Ford pickup Harry had ever seen and stumbled out, his face white.

"What happened, what happened? Is she alright?"

"She's safe, Tom, but she took a bullet in her shoulder," said Kate. "We think she was hit by a stray. She's going to be fine. Constable Fell is taking her to the hospital in Palmerston North, and they'll look after her there."

"Tom and I will come to Palmerston," said Mrs. Hardy. "Tom, I'll go in the police car with Constable Fell. You drive the lorry. You know where the hospital is, don't you?"

Tom nodded wordlessly, ready to be told what to do.

Harry exchanged a look with Kate. Thank God her grandmother was leaving. He didn't want to be responsible for two women, one of whom was in her eighties and living in a fantasy world from the past.

"What about the cows?" asked Tom. "Who's going to milk them? And who'll ride your horse, Miss Hardy? Will you be staying overnight?"

"We'll take care of that," said Kate. "I'll telephone one of our neighbors to take care of them for a day or so. You stay with Betty."

Tom bit his lip. He was shaking, about to cry.

"It's because we're Jewish, isn't it?"

Kate glanced at Harry. She seemed unsure how to answer.

"I doubt that's the case," he said. "There are a lot of crazy people out there, Tom, but I think it was likely someone out hunting who let off a wild shot. He'll be long gone by now, especially if he knows he hit someone."

They watched as the police car left, Betty reclining on the rear set, her head on Mrs. Hardy's lap, followed by Tom in the truck.

"Do you think the shooter has left?" Kate asked.

"Probably not, but let's get inside before he tells us."

He was leaning forward to open the door for her when he heard something hit the wall with a loud thump. A splinter hit him on the cheek, and Kate screamed.

He grabbed her by the arm and threw her inside. She fell on the floor; he dropped beside her and pulled the door shut.

"Did he hit you? Are you okay?"

She crawled away from the door and sat with her back to the wall.

"I felt the bullet go past my ear."

"We have to get out of here, Kate. Right now. My bike is behind the house in a ditch. Is there a rear door?"

"No. We can use the kitchen window. But by the time you get your bike, he'll be here. I bet he's running down the hill or through the paddock. Should we run for it? We can't fight him."

"Pity we don't have a weapon, but…"

"We had to hand our guns into the police at the start of the … wait, we do have a weapon," she said. "My grandfather's old rifle is in the bedroom on the wall."

"The old Enfield?" he asked. "Can we fire that? It must be a hundred years old. And what about cartridges?"

"I think there are a couple in the case. Wait here, I'll get it."

She scrambled into the bedroom on her knees, and he heard the glass smash on the case. A minute later, she returned, the rifle in hand.

"Do you know how to load it?"

"Yep. I fired it once when I was a kid. Watch out the window to make sure he isn't on the way down. He'll have a harder time aiming now that it's dark."

He squatted beneath the window and raised himself above the sill, trying to focus on the pathway that came down beside the paddock. He could hear her loading the gun behind him. "No sign of him yet."

"Alright, I got it loaded."

"Show me how to use it. Then go out the kitchen window and find my bike. It's about fifty yards away, in the ditch. I'll cover you."

"No. I'm the one who knows how to use it. I'll cover you." She crawled over to the window, holding the gun pointed at the ceiling. "I'll shoot, you get the bike. I have two shots ready. I'll

THE GUNSHOT

shoot once now and a second time when I hear you let me know you're in place."

No time to protest. "Right," he said. "Good idea. Try not to kill him. I want him alive."

10

On the Run

Kate Hardy could feel the spirit of her grandfather guiding her. She crouched on the floor, the Enfield resting on the sill of the open window, staring down the long barrel at the old seat on the ridge Granddad Frank had built so many years ago. Soon after she'd knelt by the window and positioned the ancient rifle, she'd seen a tiny flash of metallic light in the area of the seat, and she was positive the shooter was there, not in the paddock or the lane coming down the hill. It was the perfect place to target someone. All the shooter needed to do was get her in his sights, and he would have a clear shot. She was making sure that he would not get that shot, keeping her head low, staying still, and focusing on her breathing as she always did in competitions.

The seat had always been a special place for her, a place she could go to when she was unhappy or upset, a place to read her favorite books. That a killer hoped to target her from her beloved seat enraged her. Harry had said she should send a warning shot, but if her shot hit the bastard, she'd be perfectly happy.

She heard a scraping sound from the kitchen as Harry eased the window open. "Shoot when you're ready," he said. "I've got the window open, and I can see my bike."

"I'm ready. Go."

As he leaped through the window, she squeezed the trigger and braced herself for the recoil. When it came, the butt of the rifle punched against her shoulder, and she knew she was going to have a nasty bruise. But she didn't care. The pain would keep her angry and strong.

From up on the ridge, silence. She knew she'd fired close to where he lay, although she probably hadn't hit him in the darkness. But she was sure she'd come close enough to make him think twice about coming down the lane towards the cottage. She'd gained them a couple of minutes.

Harry had said to let him know they were armed. "He needs to understand there's someone here with a weapon who'll retaliate if he tries anything."

She waited, watching, her eyes adjusting to the darkness. If he decided to come down towards the cottage, she would see him. If he went back along the ridge, he might spot Harry getting his bike and take a shot at him, and she was ready to shoot again if he did. She trusted Harry to stay in the shelter of the hedge, but he would be in the open when he started the bike.

She felt a cold sweat forming on her neck, even though she had borrowed one of Betty's thick wool cardigans.

The seconds ticked away as she waited for something to happen. This must be what war was like. Not knowing what was going to happen next, living in the moment, not worrying about the possibility of your own death.

She heard the roar of the bike and aimed to the right of the seat, two feet above the top of the ridge. He would be near the seat now, not on it, probably lying flat on the ridge.

The bike stopped near the window. "Kate. Get out here."

She let off the second shot, dropped the Enfield on the floor, and ran into the kitchen. Harry was astride his bike, the engine ticking over. She went out the window feet first and jumped on behind him.

He gunned the engine. "Hang tight. Where are we heading?"

She tilted her chin onto his shoulder so she could yell into his ear.

"Turn around and go straight ahead. Turn left at the first turn, then right on the main road at the bottom of the hill. That'll take us to Feilding."

He complied but angled his head slightly and yelled back. "What's in Feilding?"

"Granny's cottage; we can hide there while we work out our next move. He'll assume we're headed to Palmerston."

He nodded and leaned forward. She clung to his back, hoping not to fall off, as the familiar fields rushed past them. It was like riding a horse, but faster.

They reached Feilding in record time. She was cold but exhilarated. When this stupid war was over, she was going to buy herself a motorcycle. She would have it painted pale green or yellow and drive around the countryside, showing herself off. She wasn't sure what that would prove, but she was extremely tired of being bossed around by men.

She'd been planning to go to Granny's cottage, but the sight of the racecourse gave her a better plan.

"Go that way. I have an idea."

He swerved left and then right and stopped in front of the

Denbigh Hotel in the center of town at her command. He turned and grinned at her.

"Are we getting a room? Works for me."

She ignored him. "Don't you think this would be the obvious place to look if he realizes we're coming to Feilding?"

"I guess so. Are we looking for the obvious? Wouldn't the cottage be a harder place for him to track us down than the hotel?"

"I was thinking we could lay a false scent," she said. "Like they do in fox hunting."

"How are we going to do that?"

"We'll get a room at the Denbigh. I'll ask for my usual room — I stay here when I come to the races, and they know me. I'll say Granny is going to pay for it and ask them to send her the bill to make sure they know exactly who I am."

He nodded. "Okay. And then?"

"Then we mess up the room, climb down the fire escape, and go to Granny's cottage. It'll delay him quite a bit."

"I'm not sure we should hang around this town," he said. "It's small, and if people know you, it won't be hard for him to find us."

"Just for the night. We can take turns watching the hotel from the cottage."

"Do we have a third bolt hole? Wouldn't the folks at the hotel know about the cottage?"

"I thought of that as we came past the race course. If we see him going into the hotel, we can leave the cottage and go to the race course, which is right behind the cottage. We can borrow a couple of horses and ride back to the farm. Then we'll have a car — two cars because the Packard is there."

His smile was broadening as she spoke. "They should send

you off to Europe to work with General Eisenhower."

"You like my plan then?"

"Other than the part where we ride back to the farm. I've never ridden a horse in my life. Is it difficult?"

"Well, yes, it is, but we can ride together on one horse, like we did on your bike. And we can take a trail I know through the bush that's too narrow for a car."

"Good. So let's go get a room."

He parked his bike beside the hotel, partly concealed by trees, hidden, but not enough not to be found by a searcher, and followed her into the hotel.

She knew booking a room would be the hardest part of her plan because they would think she was bringing in an American soldier for the night like a cheap trollop. After the war was over, she'd never be able to stay here again but would have to find a room in another hotel. And all the racing people in Feilding would hear about her and look at her sideways. But she didn't care.

Fortunately, the manager had retired to his quarters, and the night desk clerk, who she'd never met, was on duty. Even so, he looked askance at her when she asked for a room with Harry standing behind her.

"A single room?" he asked, flipping over the pages of his register as he stared at her over the top of his glasses. "Two single rooms, perhaps?"

"One double, please," she insisted. "My name is Kate Hardy. I'm Sam Hardy's daughter. My grandmother, Mrs. Mette Hardy, has a standing account here."

He nodded, recognizing the names. She could see the words, *Does your father know what you're up to?* Written in his eyes, but his finger landed on a number.

We have a room on the third floor. A suite. I believe it's the one your family usually uses. Would that suit?"

"Yes, please. And can you put it on my grandmother's account, please?"

He sighed loudly. "Of course, madam. Is there anything else you need?"

Harry stepped forward and put one hand on Kate's shoulder. "Could you send up some sandwiches? And a couple of bottles of beer as well."

"Sorry, sir, the bar is closed."

"Do you have any Coca-Cola?"

The desk clerk sighed. "Only in the bar, if at all," he said.

"Just the sandwiches then, I guess," said Harry. "What a country."

"Is that enough of a trail?" he asked as he pulled the door of the lift shut.

"I hope so," she said. "Will we have time to eat the sandwiches?"

"Who knows, but I'm starving. As soon as the food comes, we'll go down the fire escape and take the sandwiches with us."

She unlocked the door, relieved that they were safe for now. She turned to say something to him and found him standing right in front of her, his hands on his hips.

"We've got a couple of minutes. I think it's time to tell me the truth, don't you?"

"What truth? Do you think I'm hiding something from you?"

"I was warned to stay away from you, and everywhere I turn, someone mentions your father as if he's someone I shouldn't cross. Even the desk clerk knew his name. Who the hell is he? Some kind of mob boss or what?"

She stared back at him, unable to look away, wondering how

much to tell him.

"What's a mob boss?"

He grabbed her by the shoulders and stared into her eyes. "I need to know, Kate. Can I trust you, or should I leave you somewhere?"

"Of course, you can trust me. I didn't want you to know, but he's with the government."

His grip loosened, and he frowned.

"The government? I don't get it. Why wouldn't you want me to know that?"

"He wouldn't approve of an American interfering in our business. And he'd be annoyed with me for getting involved."

"What's it to him? My government has an agreement with yours. Everyone's on board with it. Tell him from me it's none of his damn business."

"He's the chairman of the Special War Cabinet," she said. "So it is his business."

"The War Cabinet? Well, I guess that makes sense. I report to the S.I.B. My contact there told me to stay away from you. He seemed to know something about you. I thought you must be a spy."

"My father isn't connected to the S.I.B.," she said. "He has a military background. I don't know why your contact would say that to you."

She did, of course, but she'd told him enough for now.

He seemed satisfied with her explanation, relieved, almost. He opened the door and looked down the hallway.

"The elevator's on the way up. Our sandwiches, I hope."

"What if it's the shooter?"

He put his finger to his lips and went out the door, closing it quietly behind him.

She turned out the light and leaned against the door. She could feel her knees trembling. It was all too much to manage. Someone trying to kill her for no reason she could think of, a murder victim on a beach that everyone seemed to have forgotten about, and an American Marine major who had taken charge of her life.

She heard voices in the hallway, and then someone tapped softly on the door.

"It's me."

She opened the door an inch and peered out. Harry was standing there with a plate of sandwiches.

"I took these from him as he got out of the elevator."

She opened the door, relieved.

He handed her a sandwich. "Eat up. The desk bell rang, and he went down to see who it was. He says he never gets people coming in this late. We need to get out of here."

She climbed through the window and followed him down the fire escape, accidentally dropping most of her sandwich and the white linen napkin it was wrapped in as she negotiated the steps. She saw the napkin land on the tin roof of a shed at the back of the hotel. Pity, but the hotel would have to do without a napkin. And with luck, there might be some sweets or potato chips at the cottage.

The fire escape ended ten feet from the ground, with a ladder that could be wound down with a hand pedal for the last ten feet, a slow and difficult process. Harry didn't wait but hung from the bottom step and dropped to the ground. She was sure he'd offer to catch her if she jumped, but she said nothing, hanging from the bottom step and dropping immediately after he had righted himself.

He caught her anyway.

The cottage was in darkness. No one at home. That worry had been in the back of her mind because Granny had so many relatives and was generous with her homes. She found the key under a pot near the front door and unlocked the door.

The cottage was dark, with a faint, musty smell.

"Don't turn the lights on," said Harry. "Our eyes will adjust to the dark."

He went to the window and looked out, keeping himself to one side.

"There's a vehicle outside the hotel. A Jeep. Must be the person who rang the bell."

Kate was feeling her way along the wall to the kitchen. She stopped and went over to join him at the window. She could see the Jeep parked near the hotel steps.

"A Jeep. I've seen one of those somewhere earlier today."

"Where? Do you remember?"

"At Massey College. I haven't had a chance to tell you, but the man you saw me speaking with at the internment camp told me a group of men had been there talking to the fugitives right before they escaped. One of them was a professor from Massey College — that's in Palmerston."

"Yeah, I rode by there earlier."

"Well, after I spoke to the professor at Massey College, I almost ran into a Jeep as I left. And I thought he seemed familiar. I thought for a minute it was you."

"And it was a military Jeep. They were built when the war started. How about the New Zealand Army? Do they have any?"

"Not that I know of. We started seeing them last year when the first Americans arrived."

Something was jiggling around in the back of her mind. She had seen the driver of the Jeep before. Where was it?

"Do you think he was a soldier? Or a Marine?"

"Oh God. Of course. He was leaving the base. Remember that man who gave you a thumbs-up at the gate?"

He shrugged. "I wasn't paying much attention. Why would he give me a thumbs-up? Do you think he recognized me?"

She wasn't sure how to answer. "Well, he was looking at me..."

He nodded slowly. "A 'You lucky dog' thumbs up, then?"

She nodded, avoiding his eyes.

"I was annoyed with him, and I glared at him. And when I saw him at the College, I think he recognized me."

He stared at the hotel, thinking.

"Get down."

He dropped to the floor, pulling her down with him.

"I saw a shadow on the bottom of the fire escape. He was leaning over towards the shed."

"It's him then. He got here pretty quickly."

"We'll have to go to the race course right now. Is there a back window?"

"In the kitchen. Same as Betty and Tom's place."

As they climbed out the back window, she had another thought.

"The man I spoke to at the internment camp is — or was — the steward at this race course. And his brother works there as well. He's a groom. He should be at the stables early in the morning to take the horses out for a gallop. We can wait there overnight and ask to borrow one."

"Better than stealing one, I guess," said Harry. "Listen, you go ahead and wait for me at the stables. I won't be long."

"What are you going to do?"

"Tell you when I get back. If I'm gone more than twenty

minutes, take a horse and ride like hell for the farm. Then drive to the nearest police station."

"I don't want to leave you here to die alone."

He squeezed her shoulder. "I'm not going to die without a hell of a fight. And I'll take him with me, believe me."

She stared up at him, blinking. She wasn't going to cry now, was she? Surely not. She hardly ever cried. Why now?

He put his hands on either side of her face, pulled her to him, and kissed her firmly on the lips, just for a minute.

"See you round."

She watched him go out the door, scarcely able to breathe.

Damn him. The last thing she'd wanted to do was to fall for an American, especially not this American, but now she knew she was going to be like Granny, still thinking and talking about the same man fifty years after she met him.

11

The Jeep

Harry crouched low in the shadows and moved slowly along a line of trees that ran between the cottage and the hotel, knife in hand, circling from side to side, looking for any enemy hidden near the hotel. He had no reason to think anyone was out here, but someone had come down the fire escape, and a second person had leaned out the window, watching him. What made him more suspicious was that the shooter had come straight to this hotel, seeming to assume they would come here even before Kate had suggested they come here. Someone must have been in Feilding waiting for the shooter. No other way to explain it.

He left the shelter of the trees and came out under the light of a single streetlight that cast long shadows across the road. He straightened up, walked briskly over to the Jeep, and rolled underneath. No doubt that it was an American military Jeep, he could tell from the series of numbers, letters, and stars painted in square white lettering along the front bumper. He memorized the numbers. Every number on a Jeep was unique, showing where it was positioned and who was likely at the wheel, almost like a fingerprint.

He had intended to slash the tires but had forgotten how thick they were. The Jeep was built to drive over the most difficult terrain, and the tires were made of extra-thick rubber. He worked away at one of the tires until he had caused a slow leak. It would take some time before it was too flat to drive, making holes big enough to cause a slow leak but not big enough to deflate them instantly. He was about to roll out when he heard a click from the front door of the hotel as it was unlocked from inside.

A minute later, the door closed with a thump, and someone tapped down the steps. Sounded like a woman. Her booted feet moved past the wheels of the Jeep and off down the street. He lay on his belly and watched her as she walked away from the hotel, a tall woman wearing a military-style camel coat belted at the back and high-heeled ankle boots: not someone who'd just finished a shift in the kitchen. Why the hell was she leaving the hotel in the middle of the night? Had she been there for an assignation? Could she have been the second shadow above the fire escape? Seemed unlikely. She wasn't trying to hide but walked confidently away as if it wasn't the first time she had been there.

A car started in the distance, and the sound of the motor slowly faded away. He rolled out from beneath the Jeep and hustled back to the darkness of the bush. His bike was leaning against a tree, and he pushed it further into the darkness, hoping to make it seem that he'd ridden off on it. He walked away regretfully, wondering if he'd ever see his Indian again. He'd spent several month's pay on the damn thing, and he loved it like a woman.

Talking of women, he'd told Kate to leave if he wasn't at the racecourse in twenty minutes, and it had been at least that long since he'd left her outside the rear window of her grandmother's cottage. She'd wait longer than twenty minutes, wouldn't she? It would be worse if she was gone. How would he know if she was safe? He was feeling way too responsible for her; it had made him lose his edge. He'd begun thinking about her safety before he embarked on a task.

He ran through the bush to the cottage. Everything was wide open, lights blaring. The window beside the front door had been smashed. The bastard had been there already while he was slashing the tires. The desk clerk must have told him where to come.

From the direction of the hotel, a car started and revved up angrily. The tires wouldn't be flat yet, still firm enough for him to drive for an hour or two. Eventually, the Jeep would lose balance as the tires on the right side became much softer than the tires on the left side. With luck, the imbalance would send him into a ditch somewhere far from the nearest town.

Now, he was worried. He plunged through the bush towards the stables, pushing aside branches, not caring about making a noise. At the race track, every building was in darkness. Had the killer been here as well? The stables were near the fence surrounding the race course, and he vaulted over the fence and ran to the open doorway. A short hallway with stalls on either side was lit by moonlight coming through the wooden wall slats and gaps in the roof.

He could hear horses snickering and shuffling around, but there was no sign of Kate. He walked softly between the stalls, knife in hand, looking for her. He was sure the enemy had left town, but he couldn't take a chance. Had he taken Kate with him? Surely he hadn't had time for that?

She wasn't there.

He whispered tentatively, "Kate?"

No reply. He took a few steps forward and said more loudly. "Katie?"

She came at him from the darkness of an empty stall so quickly that he barely had time to lower his knife, almost knocking him down and clinging to him like a limpet, her eyes wide with terror.

He pushed her away gently, relieved she'd disobeyed his instructions.

"You were supposed to leave if I didn't come back in twenty minutes."

She took a step backward, her face pink. "I'm sorry to get so panicky, but I was sure you were dead. I didn't know what to do. I wanted to come and look for you, but I didn't have the courage."

"The killer's gone. He took off in his Jeep. But I saw two shadows on the fire escape. It could've been the desk clerk helping him out, but I couldn't tell for sure. The shadow at the bottom of the fire escape was leaning forward, looking at something. Could he see the cottage or the stables from up there? I didn't notice."

She bit her lip. "I dropped my sandwich on the roof of the shed. The white napkin was showing up in the dark. Perhaps he was looking at that, wondering what it meant. I don't think he could see the cottage or the stables. The trees are huge. What are we going to do now? Huddle in a stall until my friend, the groom, gets here?"

"Is he someone you trust?"

She nodded. "Well, as much as I can trust anyone. Should I distrust everyone but you?"

He shrugged. "I think so. How far is it to the farm?"

"About five miles. Why?"

"We shouldn't wait for your pal. We should leave now and walk unless you feel okay about helping yourself to a horse."

"He'll be here in three hours. No, I'd rather not take a horse without asking him. They're quite valuable, some of them, and my father would be humiliated if I ended up in prison because I stole a horse."

"Well then, shall we walk?"

She sighed. "I was looking forward to riding, but I suppose I could manage to walk. Five miles isn't that much."

"Stay here while I'll do a recon of the area. I won't be long."

"I'm not bloody well staying by myself. Either we just go, or I recon with you. What's a recon, by the way?"

"Reconnaissance. Checking out the region to see if there are enemies present."

"You said he'd gone. Look, I'm so tired I can hardly keep my eyes open. I'll manage the five-mile walk, but if I collapse on the way to the farm, roll me into a ditch and let me sleep."

"You got it. We can hit the sack as soon as we reach the farm."

"I hope that means go to bed," she said. "Because I'm not hitting any sacks or anything else that sounds weird."

He suppressed a grin. He wasn't the only one who found the other speaker's language strange. Why didn't everyone speak like Americans? It would make their lives much easier. What would it take to get them to change? More American shows on the radio?

"Let's go then. Follow me. We'll hightail it around the outside of the race course and head along the track. Tell me where it starts."

"I have to go first. I know the way."

He surveyed the area briefly, then caught up to her. It was still dark and shadowy, but the moon had come out, and a million stars glittered above them. On the far side of the race course, yet another stand of magnificent trees. The Marine Corps had been sent here with the understanding that the terrain would be similar to places they were about to attack. He couldn't imagine the Solomon Islands would be as nice as this. Of course, the beach below Camp Russell hadn't exactly been idyllic.

They hiked along a tree-covered track for an hour, not speaking, making good progress when she stopped suddenly and bent over, clutching her side.

"I have a stitch. I need to rest."

"We can't stop," he said. "He might have enough air in his tires to get to the farm, and I want to be there well before him. Why don't I carry you?"

She straightened up, her hand on her waist, frowning.

"Carry me? How? Like a baby in your arms? I weigh eight and a half stone."

He bent over, hands on knees. "Hop on my back. I don't know how much eight and a half stone is, but you don't look too heavy to me. When I was taking the Officer Candidate Course at Quantico, I had to carry the heaviest man in my squad for two miles at double time and then get him over a wall. I think I can manage you for a couple of miles."

He omitted to add that it was ten years since he'd been at Quantico, but he was in good shape and thought he could carry her. Anything to get them to the farm as quickly as possible.

She vaulted onto his back and put her arms around his neck. He loosened her hands and straightened up. "Try not to strangle me."

"It'd be easier for me if you had reins. What should I hold on to if I can't hold you by the neck?"

"Cross your wrists in front of me, and I'll hold your hands."

He set off at a brisk pace, not double time, but as near as he could manage without a sergeant major barking at him from the rear. Fortunately, her equestrian skills helped her stay in place, making it easier for him, and he moved along quickly, chanting the Marine marching chant in his head. It was too filthy to chant aloud, unfortunately, and he needed a free hand to chant it effectively. *This is my rifle, this is my gun...*

"Tell me about the man who shot at me," she said after a few minutes, interrupting his cadence. "Did he kill that man found on the rocks near the Marine Corps training camp?"

"I dunno. I hope it was him. I'd hate to think he wasn't the only one."

"You knew someone was out there, though, an American, didn't you? Were you sent to find him?"

"The S.I.B. asked for our help. They said a group of insurgents was forming inside the country, and they'd heard an American was here to help set it up. They wanted to know about him and the group. They asked for someone from our side to be assigned to the task. Command in Hawaii decided I was it."

"Why?"

"What do you mean why? I was the best man available."

"Have you done this kind of thing before?"

He waited for a dozen steps. Might as well tell her everything. They were in this together now. "I was brought up by my German grandparents, and I speak a low German dialect fluently. My grandparents came from Bremen, the same town that Admiral Nimitz's grandfather came from, and they knew each other; he suggested me."

"And what about the man who was killed? Who was he? Another German speaker?"

"He had a bit of German. He was a volunteer from your police force, a recent immigrant from Ireland — southern Ireland — with a German mother. We gave him a new identity as a member of the Irish Republican Army here to stir up trouble and sent him to the internment camp on Somes Island. He made sure he befriended the worst people there, and then they all got transferred up to Pahiatua while Somes was under repair. He didn't have a chance to warn us about the escape plans, unfortunately. He must have decided he should go with them."

"Was he related to the head of the S.I.B. by any chance?"

"What makes you say that? Is the head of the S.I.B. Irish? I've never met him."

"He has Irish ancestry."

"You know him?"

"Yes. He'd be upset if a relative was murdered after he sent him on the job."

"You are connected, aren't you? What about Bernard Freyberg? You know him as well. And Peter Fraser, the Prime Minister?"

She didn't reply, which he took as a yes. The track had come out of the bush at what passed for a main road around here.

"You can put me down now," she said. "We're across from the farm, and my stitch has gone."

He let go of her hands, and she slid to the ground.

"Those cows in the paddock are ours. I'd forgotten about them. They'll need milking."

"Who does it normally? Betty's husband?"

"Both of them. There are only eight, so it doesn't take long when two of them are doing it. And they milk them twice a day."

"I could milk them."

She stared at him, astonished.

"You can milk cows?"

"I grew up on a farm. Maybe it would be faster to milk them enough to get by another day and not worry about saving the milk."

"I need to go up to the house to ring my uncle to come and take care of my horse for a couple of days. He could milk as well. He knows how to do it."

"Let's make it quick then. By the time you get back, I'll have them all partly milked. Where's your car?"

"In front of the house. But let's take the Packard, so we're not recognized. It's in the barn."

"Right then. I'll get these cows done, and then I'll get the Packard started. Don't be long."

He watched as she hurried up the slope to the house. It was an odd setting, with the house up on the hill and fields on either side at a much lower level. He'd have to ask her how it got that way.

He knelt by the nearest cow and grabbed her teats. "Okay then, Bessie. Let's get you depressurized. Sorry, but the milk is going to waste. I know there's a war on, but I'm in a hurry."

He spent a few minutes on each cow and finished quickly, keeping an eye on the track up to the house. Kate hadn't appeared. Her conversation with her uncle was longer than it should be. Was she calling Hamlet Sorensen or another uncle? He should have told her not to call Sorensen. He had his suspicions about Hamlet and his travel to Bavaria.

The Packard, then. He opened the door of the barn and saw it sitting there, a large gray sedan covered in a thin film of dust, other than a brush mark on the door. He took one last look at the road and then went inside. A black cat reclined on the rear seat, staring at him malevolently. How had it got in there through a closed window?

Luckily he wasn't superstitious, although he wasn't sure if black cats meant good luck or bad luck.

He opened the rear door and scooped up the cat. He was about to toss it out onto the barn floor when he felt something sharp stick into his butt. A needle. Why a needle?

Shit. Someone had been waiting for him in the barn. He should have checked it out.

The cat slipped from his hands, and a black tide dropped over his eyes, almost like a blind being lowered. Run, Kate. Run, Kate. They're...

A sensation of falling forward, and then, nothing.

12

Uncle Joey

Kate opened the door an inch and peered out. Where on earth was Uncle Joey? He'd promised to come immediately. She should have rung Uncle Hamlet. He lived further away, but he was more reliable.

A curl of dust rose from the road, and she breathed a sigh of relief. That would be him. At least she could count on Uncle Joey not to require a long explanation. If she needed him, that was enough. He would put down his paintbrush and easel and come. Eventually.

Uncle Joey was a busy man, constantly in the middle of working on a painting commissioned by businesses like the Bank of New Zealand or Todd Motors. He'd taken ages to answer the telephone, explaining that he had been on a ladder finishing the top portion of a painting that was to be hung in a government building.

"Can you come right away?" she had asked. "I have an emergency."

"Of course, I can," he said. "I'll be there as soon as I clean the paint off my hands."

Granny and Granddad had adopted Joey when he was nine or ten years old, a young Māori boy whose parents had left him alone with his grandmother to fight Europeans. Granny had encouraged his interest in art, and now his paintings sold for thousands of pounds.

Although he could afford a new car, he drove an old 1932 Hillman Minx, a large, upright car that had trouble getting up the hill from the Feilding Road. Ten minutes after she saw the puff of dust, the nine-horsepower car chugged up in front of the house and stopped. Uncle Joey, a tall, gray-haired man with gleaming bronze skin and an erect stature, stepped out, his arms stretched out towards her, smiling broadly.

"Katie, my Katie, I haven't seen you for such a long time. Why haven't you rung me or visited me before now? You know I love to see you."

She ran down the steps, grabbed his arm, and pulled him into the house.

"I'm in a bit of trouble, Uncle Joey."

He looked at her, lips compressed, and tilted his head to one side.

"Does it have something to do with the Packard being in the ditch?"

"In the…? Where did you see that?"

"About half a mile away, near the junction. How did you manage to do that?"

"I didn't. I was here, and my Marine friend I told you about was down milking the cows in the lower paddock. The Packard was in the barn. At least, I think it was, although I didn't check."

"Perhaps he took it. I didn't see him in the paddock. I don't trust those Americans. You don't know what he wants from you, do you? Well, perhaps you do, and you don't care."

"Of course he didn't take the car ... unless he needed to chase someone. Or unless ... oh, no. Someone's taken him."

"Hop into my car, and I'll take you to the barn."

She ignored him and sprinted down the lane towards the barn. Uncle Joey yelled after her, "Wait for me. Don't go down by yourself."

She heard him start the car but kept going.

She knew in her heart that someone had taken Harry.

The field was empty, with cows milling about and chomping on the grass. The door of the barn was wide open, and for a minute, she thought he must be inside. Then she saw the fresh tire tracks. And no Harry to be seen.

Uncle Joey screeched to a stop beside her and leaned out the window.

"Careful, Katie. Don't go in there."

"The Packard's gone," she said. "And so is Harry. He must have gone into the barn after he finished with the cows, and someone was waiting for him."

"Get in the car," he said, serious for once. "I knew it was Sam's car I saw in the ditch. I'll take you to where I saw it."

As they sped from the farm and along the road towards the junction, her mind swirled with possibilities. If he'd been following someone and had driven into the ditch, he might be dead or dying. An image of him smashed against the windscreen hovered in her mind, and she tried to push it away. She could hardly breathe. If he wasn't in the car, then someone had taken him for a reason. And not a good reason.

"Hurry, please, Uncle Joey."

He managed to get his aging car up to top speed, spouting smoke, the engine screaming, and they made it to the Packard in record time. The car slowed, and she leaped out, not waiting for him to park, jumped up onto the rear wheel of the Packard, and wrenched open the door. The car was tilted at an awkward angle, and the door slipped from her hands and slammed shut. But she had seen enough to know he wasn't inside.

"Don't rock the car," said Uncle Joey. "It'll flip, and you'll hurt yourself."

He pulled a small hammer from somewhere in the Hillman and ran to the front of the car in the ditch. The windscreen shattered, and he levered himself up and looked through the hole in the glass.

"No one in there. Check the boot."

She slid to the ground and tore open the boot, even though she knew there wasn't enough room for a large man in there.

"He isn't under the car," yelled Uncle Joey. "And there are tire marks on the grass in front of the Packard. Another car was here."

They stood looking at each other.

"He was taken from the barn and brought here," said Uncle Joey. "Is he a large man?"

She nodded. "Maybe there were two people. He'd put up a fight, but I didn't see any sign of that, did you?"

"Or the kidnapper knocked him out. But it's not easy to get someone into a car when they're unconscious."

She knelt and examined the tire marks left by the other car. Was it a Jeep? Jeeps weren't very heavy. She'd read about three American soldiers lifting a Jeep into a parking spot. And all the marks looked even, with no sign of flat tires.

"Do you think these look uneven?"

Uncle Joey shook his head. "They look the same to me. What are you going to do, Katie?"

She tried to calm herself, to give herself time to think. Should she go back to the Marine base and ask for help? He was a Marine. Surely, they wouldn't ignore her pleas for assistance. Or call the police? How would she explain everything to the police?

Perhaps she should go to Massey College or the internment camp. Her trip to those places had triggered the attempt on her own life, and she'd seen the man in the Jeep at the College.

The Marine camp was out. They would make her stay there while they went in search of Harry, and she would go mad waiting for them to find him. It had to be either Massey College or the internment camp. And Massey College was closer. She could go to the internment camp if she found nothing at the College.

"I'm going to Massey College to talk to Professor Collins. He must know something."

The good thing about Uncle Joey was that he didn't insist on knowing what she was talking about. "How will you make this professor tell you anything?"

"I don't know. I could make a fuss."

"Why don't you take a gun? Don't point it at him. Just wave it around threateningly."

Kate was shocked. Uncle Joey was suggesting she do something that could get her sent to prison. "Really?"

"Or you could have a gun on your hip, but don't take it out. Just flash it at him."

"You've been spending too much time at the picture theatre, Uncle Joey. And where would I find a gun? All we have is Granddad's old Enfield. They'll think I'm crazy if I walk in with that."

"I have a friend in Palmerston who collects guns," he said. "Get in the car, and we'll see if he's at home."

"You mean he collects old guns?" She was open to the idea of scaring Professor Collins, but not with an antique weapon. "I don't need another old gun."

"They're not old," said Joey. "He buys them cheap from return soldiers who've taken them off dead Germans. He thinks they'll be worth a lot eventually."

She'd heard about soldiers looting bodies after a battle but hadn't realized it was for guns. She'd assumed they were looking for food or clothing. Maybe she had the wrong war in mind.

"Alright then. Let's go and visit your friend."

Visiting Uncle Joey's friend was not as straightforward as she thought it would be. They parked the car down a dark alleyway and walked quietly around a corner to an unlit house. Uncle Joey knocked on the door with what sounded like a secret knock, and a man with long wild hair and a long beard answered and ushered them inside.

"What's up, Joe? Is this your new girlfriend?"

"This is my niece, Kate," said Uncle Joey. "Look, Damien, Kate needs a gun to wave at someone. Do you have one we could buy or borrow? Something scary looking."

Damien eyed Kate up and down. "You can borrow my Luger if I can come with you when you use it. I want to see what happens when you wave a Luger around. But I can't let you take it by yourself. It's my prize weapon. It was taken off a dead German at the battle of El Alamein. In Egypt, you know? All the blokes coming home wounded are bringing Lugers with them if they can get hold of one. Great weapon. Better than anything the Yanks have."

Uncle Joey glanced at Kate. "What do you think, Katie? If the gun doesn't scare the professor, Damien will," he said. "Are you alright if Damien comes with you?"

"But not if you're planning to kill someone," said Damien. "I draw the line at that. I can't get arrested again. What did he do to you? Something nasty?"

Kate managed to answer as if they were discussing how they were going to arrange the flowers in church for a wedding.

"I don't want to kill him. I just need some information from him."

"Hmm." Damien thought about it, then nodded. "I have a nice semiautomatic pistol I can sell you. A .45 caliber Colt 1911. The Yanks use them, so they're not too bad. And I can sell you a holster for it as well. It used to belong to a general. Very fine leather."

"Can we have a look at the gun?" asked Uncle Joey.

Damien left the room, and they heard him fumbling around in the next room.

Kate was beginning to feel anxious. She had to find Harry soon before the killer did something to him, but she wanted to be armed. If she didn't use the pistol to intimidate Professor Collins, she'd need it to rescue Harry. Damien had got her worried, asking her if she intended to kill someone.

Damien returned with a tea towel draped over his open palm, a gun resting on it.

"Here it is. Can you shoot, Kate? I can give you a lesson if you want."

"I was All Round Champion at the Manawatu Rifle Club shooting contest two years in a row," she said. "I think I can manage a pistol."

He stroked the gun as if it were a steel gray cat rather than a dangerous weapon.

"I'll need fifty quid for it."

She had a ten-pound note in her pocket, her emergency cash, but it would take days to raise fifty pounds. Her heart sank.

Uncle Joey pulled out a massive wallet and started peeling off notes. "One, two, three, four, five ... there you go."

Damien took them and shoved them into his pocket, grinning happily. He'd made a nice profit, Kate thought.

"What about the holster?" she asked.

He disappeared again and returned carrying a holster on a belt and a hammer and nail. "This will be too big for you. The general was a hefty bloke. I'll put another hole in the belt so it doesn't fall off you."

When they were finally back in the Hillman, Kate belted the holster around her waist and buckled it up. It fit very nicely and made her feel she could take on anyone.

"Cowgirl Kate," said Joey. "It hardly shows under your coat. If you put your hand on your hip with the coat sort of pulled back, he'll see it. That'll do the trick, especially if you curl your lip while you're doing it."

"Uncle Joey, can I borrow your car for a few hours? I'll drop you off at the Royal Hotel. I think Granny will be there, and she'd love to see you."

"I haven't seen Mama for weeks," said Joey. "Yes, leave me there and take the car. Try not to wreck it. I know I need another one, but I'm happy with this one. I'll have to tell Mama that someone put her car in the ditch as well, but she's pretty relaxed about that sort of thing after the life she's had with Sergeant Frank."

"And thank you so much for paying for the gun. I'll pay you back as soon as I can."

He shrugged. "No worries. You're going to get it all anyway. You may as well have some of it early."

She leaned over and kissed him on the cheek. "I'll give it all to a children's charity. But you have a good twenty years left in you, so I'm not planning how to spend it yet."

"Mama will leave you everything as well. You're going to be the richest girl in New Zealand in a few years."

He was probably right, but it made her feel uncomfortable. She'd rather make money herself. If she inherited the farm and a little money, she'd be happy for the rest of her life. Maybe she'd be a little happier if Harry was there with her, but she wasn't going to think about that yet. She had to save his life first.

She dropped Uncle Joey off at the Royal Hotel without waiting to speak with Granny and continued towards Massey College. Harry had been gone for over an hour, and her anger at the person who had taken him was growing. Professor Collins had better tell her something useful, or she didn't know what she would do. The gun nestled against her hip, feeling as if it was where it belonged.

Thank goodness Uncle Joey had friends in low places.

13

The Captive

He woke an endless time later with a rubber tube down his throat and something dripping down into his stomach. He could see a funnel at the end of the tube, suspended on the railing at the head of the bed. He was being force-fed something that was intended to knock him out or kill him. Alcohol of some kind, and with no taste or smell.

Grain alcohol.

He couldn't tell how much he'd swallowed, but he was already feeling cold, and he wanted to vomit. He suppressed the urge, lying as calmly as he could, flat on his back and breathing in and out through his nose, trying to let some of the liquid dribble out the side of his mouth.

He worked his tongue on the tube and gradually eased it up. When the end of the tube was in his mouth, he coughed it out, gagging. It slid across his cheek and onto the cot.

It left a burning trail across his cheek, and he was overcome with nausea. Vomiting would be the best thing. He'd been at a dance in his youth where he'd been offered grape juice laced with grain alcohol and tossed it back to show he could handle it.

He'd had no idea how toxic it was. After one glass, he'd thrown it all up. Still took a couple of days to get over it, though.

He strained his head over until the side of his face was pressed against the pillow and forced himself to retch until his stomach was empty.

Then, with his face still lying in vomit, he fell into a deep, dreamless sleep.

The first thought that crossed his mind when he came to again was that he'd been paralyzed by the grain alcohol. He was on a cot, unable to move anything but his head, his body immovable. Had the grain alcohol done that? Or was it something else? The tube was draped across his chest, and the contents of the funnel spilled onto his shirt. He'd ingested more than he realized, and it had paralyzed him. He hoped to God it wasn't permanent.

Then he retched again and realized he could move his neck and shoulders. His body was still functioning, but he was trussed up like a Thanksgiving turkey, tied down by the wrists and ankles with heavy leather straps, with a thin gray army blanket tucked tightly under his chin and down beneath the mattress. Difficult to move. Swaddled.

He opened his eyes slightly, not wanting anyone to know he was awake. Shadows moved outside a window in the door of a dimly lit room, but the room itself was empty, and there was just a single, glazed window in the door, nothing on the walls. A hospital room, but not a hospital ward. More like a sick bay, he thought, with three other cots, all empty.

Should he shout, or would that just bring whoever it was who'd brought him here?

He dropped his chin to his chest, which felt strangely bare. His dog tags had been removed, the tags that identified him as

Major Harry Wilhelm. No military hospital would remove dog tags. He had to find out where he was and figure out how he could get away. The first thing he had to do was free himself from the straps. If he could free himself from one, he could undo the rest easily.

He lay and took several deep breaths, flexing his arms and legs to increase circulation. He was feeling the aftereffects of the drug that had been injected into his butt. Whoever had done it didn't want him dead, or he wouldn't be lying here, but they sure wanted him incapacitated. Maybe they wanted him dead but in the right place, and a barn belonging to the Chairman of the Special War Cabinet wasn't it. The entire police force would be out looking for his killer if he'd been left in the barn beside the Packard. If he died here of alcohol poisoning, they could dump his body somewhere and make him look like a drunken hobo. No one would bother finding out how he died.

His left wrist would be easier to free. He was right-handed, and his left wrist was a fraction smaller than his right. He started with a straight tug, but that drew blood without freeing him. All four straps holding him down had buckles; if he wiggled his wrist from side to side slowly, the strap through the buckle lifted slightly.

He lay, keeping calm, moving his wrist from side to side, and eventually, he felt a slight pop. The buckle was halfway undone. Eager to get it off, he jerked his arm back and heard the buckle engage again.

Patience, Wilhelm, he said to himself. He lay still until he had control of his breathing and started again. The next time the end lifted, he rubbed it very gently against the mattress until it came completely undone.

No need for patience. He threw off the strap on his left wrist and undid the other strap awkwardly with his left hand. Once that was off, he could free his legs. Leaning forward to undo the straps on his ankles, he felt a momentary blackness come over him, leaned back until it had gone, and then returned to the ankle straps.

He slid off the cot and was surprised to discover that his legs wouldn't support him. He'd lost strength in his thighs and calves. He dragged himself upright using the frame of the cot and did some deep knee bends. When he felt his strength returning, he made his way carefully around the room. He was wearing a hospital gown, and his feet were bare. No boots, no knife.

He opened a metal closet and found his clothing folded neatly on the upper shelf. The boots were sitting on a lower shelf, but the knife was gone. He put on his clothes and boots and went to the door. It was locked, of course, and the glass was opaque. He would have no problem battering it open, but that would draw the enemy, whoever they were, and however many of them there were. Surely an entire hospital couldn't be filled with enemies unless he was on a ship or a submarine, but he felt no movement. He was on land. He could hear the murmur of voices not too far away. He hadn't been left in an empty hospital.

He was about to risk battering down the door when someone turned the key. He watched as the handle started to move, flattened his back against the wall, and waited. He had no weapon, but he had the element of surprise. Whoever came through that door, Harry would put him in a stranglehold and squeeze the life out of him.

A man in his fifties, his eyes wide, stumbled through the door, staring at Harry.

"She's got a ..."

Harry didn't wait. He spun the man around and put his arm across the man's throat.

"Okay then, you Nazi bastard. Where the hell am I, and what do you want with me?"

14

Return to Massey College

The receptionist at the desk at Massey College looked at Kate, puzzled. She was a woman in her fifties, with soft gray hair pulled back in a bun and glasses hanging on a chain.

"I'm sorry, dear. But I don't remember you being here before."

"It was just a couple of days ... oh, wait. Now I come to think of it, another woman was at the reception desk. She was younger than you and had dark hair pulled back."

The receptionist's face cleared. "Oh, that must have been Lina. She was waiting for her friend to pick her up. I was eating my lunch in the canteen. She should have called me, really, but she thinks she's my superior."

Kate nodded vaguely. She'd run into feuding secretaries before and had no intention of taking a side.

"Well, anyway, I asked to speak to Professor Collins, and then I went around the back where he was throttling chickens. Is he in? Could I speak to him?"

The woman adjusted her cardigan, which was draped over her shoulders, and put her glasses on so she could look over them.

"Throttling chickens? Are you sure he wasn't feeding them?"

"Quite sure. Is he here today?"

"I believe he's gone to meet with poor Dr. Klein again. He's very interested in his theory ... I'm not sure what theory, exactly ... but it has something to do with breeding new variations. And Dr. Klein is so happy to see him because his life is dreadfully dull in the camp."

"The camp? Dr. Klein is in the internment camp in Pahiatua?"

"Pahiatua? I'm not sure. I know Dr. Klein was going across the ranges because he hates driving through the Gorge and complained about it before he left, but he wanted to see him. You'd think a man of such high distinction wouldn't be interned."

Got him, thought Kate.

"You can talk to Professor Collins when he returns later today. I'll give you his telephone number if you like."

Kate pulled out a pencil from her purse and rummaged around for a piece of paper. Why had she given away her notebook? She couldn't live without it.

"Are you looking for paper? Use the back of this pamphlet."

Kate took the pamphlet and glanced at it before turning it over. Something about a Eugenics Society. Typical of this institution, which seemed to be overrun with Nazis.

"I'm ready. What was the telephone number?"

The receptionist flipped through a card file on the corner of her desk and read the number to Kate.

"Thank you. If he returns here, don't mention that I was looking for him. I'm not sure if I have time to go to ring him, and I don't want him to be disappointed."

She folded the page in half and was about to stuff it into her purse when a name jumped out at her from the front of the pamphlet.

H. Sorensen. On the committee. The treasurer of the Eugenics Society.

Uncle Hamlet. What was he doing as a member of the Eugenics Society? And what was a Eugenics Society about, come to that? Why did they need to meet regularly? Could they possibly be the group Harry was looking for, meeting harmlessly while working against the country? But that would mean Uncle Hamlet was a traitor, which was unthinkable.

"What does this group do?" she asked, waving the pamphlet at the receptionist.

The receptionist made a shrugging gesture with her lip and one shoulder.

"Search me. Something to do with sterilizing mental defectives and sexual offenders. The government ran an inquiry into it before the war and discovered that the feeling in the country was against it. Professor Collins wants them to take another look because of what we've learned about inherited traits."

Kate felt her lip curl and rubbed her nose to hide it. They sounded like a bunch of Nazis. What reason would Hamlet have to join such a group? Not because of his brother Jens, she hoped. Shell shock wasn't a reason to sterilize someone, was it? What harm could poor Jens do, trapped in his hut at the back of the house?

"Is Professor Klein part of this group?"

"I don't believe so. But he's very knowledgeable on the subject of eugenics, and they consult him frequently. He taught at the Kaiser Wilhelm Institute of Anthropology, Human Heredity, and Eugenics in Berlin before he came to New Zealand to teach here, and Professor Collins has been keen to recruit him to the cause. But, of course, because he's a German, he was interned, which has created a difficulty."

"Is Professor Klein still in the internment camp? Several men escaped a week ago. He wouldn't be one of them, would he?"

She frowned. "He's quite elderly. I can't imagine him climbing over the fence or crawling through a hole in the wire. I suppose you could ask Lina about that, though."

"Lina? You mean the woman who was on the desk the last time I was here? Why would she know anything?"

"She's the chairwoman of the Eugenics Society," said the receptionist. "Didn't I mention that? Her name is probably on the flier. She's meeting them at the camp today."

Something clicked into place in Kate's head. The last time she was here, she had almost crashed into a man in a Jeep when she was leaving, and Lina had been sitting at the desk, apparently waiting for someone.

"When I spoke to Lina, was she waiting for some? A man in a Jeep, perhaps?"

"She did say a military man was coming to pick her up, but she didn't mention a Jeep."

"An American, did she say?"

"I'm not sure. He's very rude, though. He was here earlier looking for her. I told him she might have gone to Pahiatua with Professor Collins just to get rid of him, even though Professor Collins was alone."

"Why would you tell him that if it wasn't true?"

"He yelled at me and called me something very unpleasant. I thought it would serve him right if he went through the Gorge and couldn't find her and had to return. Of course, he probably went on the Pahiatua track as it's closer to here and faster, and if you aren't a local, you don't know how ..."

Kate was already running out the door. All the villains were converging on the internment camp in Pahiatua, so that's where she would go. Thank God she had Damien's pistol with her. If Harry were trapped in the camp, she would shoot her way in, if necessary, to save him and deal with the consequences later. Her father would just have to put up with the shame of her going to prison.

She chugged slowly over the Pahiatua Track in the Hillman Minx, her foot flat on the pedal, wishing she was driving the Roadster and wondering if Max, her editor, had noticed she hadn't returned his car. The only way to gather any speed was by coasting down the hills. She kept her foot on the brake, but the car resisted, and she almost lost control a couple of times. Plunging off the cliff would not help her save Harry.

She was rounding a curve, using all her strength to turn the wheel, when a car came at her from the other direction in the middle of the road. She slammed on the brake, pulling on the handbrake at the same time, and steered into the bushes on the upward side of the hill.

It was the Jeep driven by the American, and he was alone.

He didn't seem to notice her, partly because Uncle Joey's car had such small windows but also because the Jeep now had two flat tires on one side, and he was struggling to maintain control.

She was on a narrow stretch of road with a steep drop on one side. She backed out onto the road and looked for a place where she could make a turn, but the drop was too close.

From behind her, a screech of tires, a panicked yell, and a series of thumps.

He had gone over the edge.

She kept going, backing around a difficult corner until she found a double line of fresh tread marks on the road. She pulled the Hillman to the far side and jumped out.

Fifteen or twenty feet from the edge of the road, its grill pressed into the dying trunk of an old rimu tree was the Jeep. The American was inside, clinging to the door, leaning back to counterbalance the slow shifting of the vehicle. The slightest movement would cause it to slip away from the rimu tree and plunge the rest of the steep scrub-covered hill with nothing to stop it for five hundred yards. From where she stood, a small farmhouse near the bottom of the hill could have been a doll's house, and a truck parked nearby resembled a child's Dinky toy you could hold in your hand.

Kate crouched on the edge of the road and yelled out to him. "Are you alright down there?"

"I can't get out without rocking the Jeep. Get help."

He sounded panicky, which, of course, he would be, facing the prospect of a long, accelerating tumble followed by near-certain death from a broken neck.

She ran back to the car to see if there was anything useful in the boot and discovered a length of coiled rope covered in paint splatters. She tied it around one of the posts on the side of the road and went over the ridge with the rope held around her waist, the way they used to do in physical education classes at high school. If she managed to tie the other end around something on the Jeep to stabilize it, he could climb out and drag himself back up to the road. He'd have to do it on his own, though. She doubted she could drag him up by herself, and she wasn't going to risk her life for someone who'd tried to kill her less than twenty-four hours ago.

Up on the road, another car had stopped; the driver yelled out to her.

"Miss, miss, help is on the way. Someone has gone to Palmerston to bring the police. Don't go any further. Stop where you are."

She was a few feet from the Jeep, but she did what she was told, clinging to a root of the rimu tree that ran up from the tree itself.

"Keep still," she said to the man in the Jeep. "The police are coming. And I'll make sure you get arrested for shooting at me."

His head moved slightly. "Kate Hardy?"

So he knew her.

"Yes, I am."

"It wasn't me. I didn't shoot at you."

"What about the body on the beach at the Marine training camp? Was that you?"

The Jeep lurched forward a few inches, and the driver grunted in terror.

She yelled back to the person who had called her from the road.

"I'm going to try and tie the rope to the Jeep. If I don't, he'll fall."

The head of the man in the Jeep moved slightly.

"Get away from me."

"I'm not here to kill you. I'm trying to help you."

"Bitch. I wish you'd been shot."

An odd way to put it. Maybe he hadn't been the one who'd shot at her. In that case, who was it?

"Where's Harry Wilhelm? If you tell me where he is, I'll throw you a rope."

"I don't know any damn Harry Wilhelm."

She moved a few inches closer and spotted a rifle on the floor below the passenger seat. He saw her looking, and he lunged for it instinctively.

"Don't do that! You'll throw it off balance."

The Jeep inched slowly sideways, and he began to scream.

Someone yelled from the road.

"Don't look, miss. He's going down."

But she had to watch. The Jeep slid from its perch and started down the hill backward. She could see his face, white with terror, as he gripped the seat, staring up at her. She couldn't see him when the Jeep started to flip slowly backward, and then it disappeared for a long minute into a dip she hadn't realized was there.

It came into view again and began to flip head over tail like a boomerang, gathering speed until it was no more than the size of a toy car. Somewhere along the way, the driver vanished, either pushed down into the Jeep or tossed from the car.

A voice above her said gently, "Come on, miss, I'll help you back up to the road. That was a nasty thing for you to see."

"Thank you. I can make it by myself."

"Was he someone you knew?"

"I've seen him around, but I don't know who he is. I wish I did. I wish I could have saved him."

"You did your best. The police will be here soon, and they'll scrape him up from somewhere down there."

A crowd had gathered on the road, and it took several minutes for her to ease the car past the onlookers and continue on her journey. Even though she knew this man might have been responsible for the murder on the rocks and her own near-death experience, she couldn't help feeling sad about his horrible death.

She arrived in Pahiatua and drove out to the camp, one of the many race tracks she had haunted before the war. She could see Uncle Hamlet's car parked outside his house and wished she hadn't seen his name on the flier. He would have helped her get into the camp and out again simply by using his charm. Everyone loved Hamlet except perhaps Helga, his wife, who was the most downtrodden woman Kate had ever met.

She parked the car outside the camp and sat staring through the wire, thinking. She could feel the gun on her hip and wondered if the guard would need to pat her down on the way in, assuming he even let her in. She couldn't take a chance of not getting inside. She had to get inside.

A memory surfaced from ten years earlier when she had been staying with Uncle Hamlet and had been a keen tree climber. She remembered she had climbed the tree almost to the top and had sat looking out over the racetrack, thrilled that she could see the horses without having to pay to get in.

She drove further along, past Uncle Hamlet's farm, and made her way around the back.

The tree was still there, its branches swaying magnificently out over a newly built barbed wire fence at the rear entrance to the race course, its trunk hard against the wire. Someone had decided that it was impossible to climb out of the camp using that tree, and in case anyone tried to climb in, they had removed all the lower branches.

She hadn't climbed a tree in years, and the memory of the unknown man in the Jeep tumbling to his death had left her shaken and nervous. But she was sure Harry was in this camp somewhere, held against his will, and she knew she would climb as high as necessary to get inside to save him.

Although the lower branches of the tree had been trimmed away, someone had made a staircase on the trunk, which had indentations that looked fresh. Wedges of wood had been shoved into each cut. She craned her neck around the tree, pushing against the wire. The cuts were on both sides of the tree. This must be how the men had escaped, and because the indentations were on the outside of the huge tree as well as on the inside, they'd had help.

The tree was on Uncle Hamlet's land.

Her heart sank. *Oh, Uncle Hamlet, what have you done?*

She reached for the remaining stump of a low branch and stepped up the tree. It was like going upstairs to bed, an easy climb up to the large branch that hung over the fence.

She sat on the branch and stared out at the camp, just as she had done when she was a girl. The old grandstand hid part of her view, but she could see the racetrack that was now used for outdoor activities and exercise. Groups of men were strolling around chatting, and over near the gate, under a shade tree, a few men were working on something smaller, carving or making ornaments. Any of them could glance her way at the wrong time and see her drop down on the inside of the fence. Would anyone report her? They'd assume she was visiting one of the men and cheer her on, most likely.

She moved forward on the branch and was about to lower herself on it when a woman in a camel coat came into view from behind the grandstand.

Lina. She was by herself and on her way out of the camp. As she walked towards the gate, she half-turned and waved at someone at the other end of the stand where the high-risk prisoners were being held in the special compound. It did not come as a surprise to Kate that Lina was visiting a high-risk prisoner. Whatever fifth-column organization Harry had been tracking, she was part of it. And someone in the high-risk area was in it with her.

Kate did not hesitate. She swung out over the fence and dropped to the ground. With her collar up and her hair tucked from sight, she strode towards the end of the stands as if she knew where she was going.

Rounding the corner, she bumped into a man coming from the other direction.

Professor Collins.

He reeled back, glaring at her.

"What the hell are you doing here?"

Kate pulled back her coat, as Joey had suggested, and revealed the pistol nestled against her hip. Professor Collins's eyes dropped to her hip and then back up to her face.

"I need you to show me where Harry Wilhelm is," she said. "I know he's here somewhere."

15

The Internment Camp

Professor Collins stared at Kate, sneering, not the least bit afraid of her. She'd thought showing him the weapon and then pulling it out and pointing it at him would have had more of an impact.

"Put that gun away, or I'll report you to the commandant," he said. "You can't wave around a gun in here. There are guards all over the place."

Kate lowered the gun until it was pointing towards his knees.

"You might have a problem getting to the commandant," she said. "I hear it's difficult to walk after you've been shot in the knee. Not just when you're fetching a guard but for the rest of your life. Major Wilhelm is in here somewhere, and I want him out. If I go to prison for shooting you in the knee, I don't care."

He pulled his coat over his knees as if that would stop a bullet.

"I don't know anyone named Major Wilhelm."

"Your lot have been trying to kill me ever since I visited you at Massey College. And they took Major Wilhelm from my family farm yesterday."

"My lot? What do you mean, my lot?"

Kate ignored his question and kept the pistol trained on his knees.

"Why are you here? Who are you visiting?"

"I came to speak with Dr. Klein, the renowned geneticist who's been interned here."

"Aren't you part of the Eugenics Society?"

"Why should I be? I'm interested in breeding chickens, not humans. What have the Eugenics Society got to do with anything?"

Kate's resolve wavered slightly, and she adjusted her hold on the pistol. The last time she'd spoken with him, he'd started to say something about the Māori people. She'd stopped him and demanded he get out of her car without waiting to hear what he'd been about to say. Perhaps she should have let him finish his sentence before she rushed to judgment.

"Have you spoken to Dr. Klein yet? Why are you wandering around out here by yourself?"

"He was already with a visitor and can only see one person at a time, so they asked me to wait out here."

"I saw her leaving a few minutes ago," said Kate. "She waved goodbye to someone in the special compound."

"Her? Who?"

"Lina."

He frowned. "Lina was here visiting Dr. Klein? Are you sure?"

"Yes, she was, but forget her. I want to find Major Wilhelm. He was snatched by someone, and he wouldn't go easily. I believe he was drugged, and I'm almost sure he's here at the camp somewhere."

Professor Collins shrugged. "Perhaps he's in the infirmary, although why anyone would..."

"Take me there," she said. "If anyone asks where we're

going, tell them we're going to the infirmary to visit a patient. We're a nurse and a doctor. Got it? I'll have my gun on you the whole time. I still don't trust you, so do as you're told."

He shrugged again. "If you insist. You won't get out of here with him, though."

She tended to agree, but one step at a time. If she found Harry in the infirmary, she could stay with him and send for the commandant. Surely, he wasn't in on any of this.

The grandstand was split into two, with an alleyway in the middle. The banks of seats had been converted into sleeping areas for the internees, with mattresses and blankets thrown onto them to create narrow beds. It looked like an awful way to live, especially in winter. And where did the high-risk prisoners sleep? Dr. Klein was a high-risk prisoner, she realized. Why was that? She'd look into that after she found Harry.

At the back of the alleyway, between the banks of seats, a swing door had once led to an office area and rooms where jockeys prepared for the races. She could imagine them pushing open the door, saddles hanging from their arms. Why did there have to be a war? Why wasn't this still a race track?

She took hold of Professor Collins's elbow and steered him through the swing doors.

"Where's the infirmary?"

"On the right. The kitchens and the staff offices are on the left. Will you let me go now? I'll go straight to my car and leave; I swear I will."

"Not until I find Major Wilhelm. Where's the special compound? Is that where Dr. Klein is being held?"

"Yes, it is. It's behind the infirmary. There's a hallway on the other side of that door leading around the outside of the infirmary. I can show you if you like."

Suddenly, he was helpful. She thought she knew why.

"Are there guards outside the entrance to the special compound?"

Professor Collins clamped his lips tight and avoided her eyes. She could tell he intended to take her to the entrance of the special compound and yell something about her being armed. She would not be able to take them all on simultaneously. She had to stop him from saying anything.

"Open the first door and then very quietly open the door to the infirmary. If you yell, I'll clock you on the head with the butt of my pistol and run for it. I might get away, but you won't know because you'll be unconscious."

He glared at her and said something in another language.

"*Du verdammte Schlampe.*"

Kate knew a little, a very little, German and Danish from her grandmother. He had called her something rude, although she wasn't sure what.

She replied with a German phrase she'd heard Granny use.

"*Achte auf deine Manieren.*"

Mind your manners.

It was enough to shut him up.

They went through the first door together. The next door they came to had the word *Infirmary* painted above the small glazed window. The key was in the lock.

"Unlock the door and push it open."

She had the pistol pressed against his head now. She had no idea what she would do if Harry wasn't inside. Lock him in the infirmary and leave the same way she came? She could do that, but then what about Harry? What if he was in a different place, like the kitchen or even the old stables?

The door creaked open. He turned to say something, but

suddenly, the handle was wrenched from his hands, and he flew inside, pulled by an unseen force. A well-muscled arm snaked around his neck, almost lifting him off his feet. He kicked out his feet, struggling for breath, his eyes bulging.

She felt a burst of happiness run through her body.

"Harry!"

"Kate? What are you doing here?"

"I came to save you. Are you alright?"

Professor Collins began to grunt and flap his arms.

Harry loosened his hold slightly.

"Should I let this guy go?"

She nodded, and he tossed him towards the cot in the center of the room. The professor landed on the bed and lay there clutching at his throat and trying to get his breath back. She saw with horror that the cot had leather straps in the corners and someone had been vomiting on the thin blanket. Harry had been there and had managed to free himself. She wanted to hold him and make him better, but, as usual, now was not the time. One of these days, it would be the right time.

She followed Professor Collins into the room and stood by the cot with her pistol trained on him. Better than flinging herself at Harry again, although she wanted to.

The professor looked up at her and gasped something in German.

"I don't speak German."

Harry replied to him in rapid German, then turned to Kate.

"He thinks we're going to kill him. Where did you get the sidearm? It's a US Army issue Colt 1911. Is it stolen?"

"I bought it from a friend of Uncle Joey. I don't know where he got it. But we have to get out of here, Harry, before anyone comes. There are guards not far away at the entrance to the special compound."

"Guards? Special compound? Where the hell am I?"

"You're in the infirmary at the internment camp in Pahiatua. Harry, I have a way to get you out, but we must leave immediately."

He nodded. "Okay then. We'll have to tie buddy here to the cot first. Who is he?"

"Professor Collins. I'm not sure why he's speaking German. His name's English and he speaks perfectly good English. He's from Massey College. Your group of traitors is connected to the college. They meet under the guise of a Eugenics Society."

Harry pulled the professor's arms back and grabbed one of the straps.

"Kolenz is a German name," he said. "Kolenz with a K. Maybe his family changed their name." He had one hand over the professor's mouth, making it hard to do up the buckles.

"Find some tape, Kate."

She kept the pistol steady and backed around the room, looking over her shoulder.

"I can't see any tape. Would a bandage do?"

"Yep. Give me your handkerchief, and I'll gag him."

"I won't yell," said the professor to Harry. "I swear I won't. Don't gag me."

Harry ignored him; he forced the professor's jaw open, stuffed Kate's handkerchief into his mouth, and then tied a bandage around his head to hold the gag in place. The professor's eyes were bulging as he kicked at the thin mattress, but he was secure for now.

"Give me the sidearm. Where are we going?"

She handed it to him reluctantly. She'd felt safe holding a pistol, but now was not the time to argue about it.

"There's a tree by the fence. I used to climb it when I was small. Someone cut steps into it for the escape, I think."

He shoved the pistol into his belt. "On Sorensen's property?"

He'd said what he had been in the back of her mind the whole time.

"You think Uncle Ham is a traitor?"

"Either him or Helga."

She felt as if a light had come on. Helga and Hamlet. They had the same initials. H. Sorensen. Could it be Helga's name on the flier and not Hamlet's? She was born in Germany, after all, and had been spat on and called names since the war began. Because of that, she seldom left home. If it was her name on the list, at least it made sense. The question was, did Hamlet know what she was up to? How could he not know?

Professor Collins was writhing from side to side and grunting.

"That won't free you," said Harry. "Might as well relax for now. Someone will come soon. Let's go then, Kate. Lead the way."

"We'll go out through the kitchen so we can keep out of sight. There's an outside door there, or there used to be."

He was opening the kitchen door for her when they heard a loud sound, halfway between a grunt and a yell, coming from the infirmary.

"He got his gag off. Let's go."

In the kitchen, a single older man was washing dishes. He dropped a plate on the floor, and it bounced under the sink. Not fine china, but some kind of plastic. Melamine, she thought, wondering why it mattered right now.

"Hey, you can't come in here."

The door at the end of the kitchen had been nailed shut, and already they could hear sounds of activity at the infirmary end of the grandstand.

"Get away from the door and cover your face," Harry said.

He threw himself against the door until it came off its hinges, the nails still in place, and then wrenched it open the rest of the way.

"Where to?"

The fence and the tree were less than a hundred yards away.

Kate was stepping through the wrecked door when a man's voice asked, "What do you think you're doing?"

Harry leaned back into the kitchen and held up his card to the commandant.

"Major Wilhelm of the US Marine Corps. I'm on a mission. Please do not interfere."

Then, to Kate, "Let's get the hell out of here."

As they reached the tree with steps, two armed guns burst through the door behind them. Harry hoisted Kate up to a lower branch and leaped up behind her. No need for the steps.

"Wish I was wearing my damned uniform," he said as they dropped to the other side. "Where's your car?"

"Along from the farm. On the road. I haven't got my car. I'm using Uncle Joey's old car. It doesn't go very fast."

"Never mind. Let's get to the nearest police station and fill them in on the situation They can contact the commandant."

"Then where?"

"Back to Palmerston," he said. "I think we're going to have to start over. The first thing we'll do is find that dammed Jeep and see who the driver is."

She couldn't run and speak at the same time. She would tell him about the man in the Jeep when they reached the police station.

16

The Pahiatua Police Station

Kate was constantly amazed at Harry's ability to put himself in charge of a situation and at how everyone genuflected towards him as if he were King George or Winston Churchill—or the Pope, if she wanted to be more accurate.

Sergeant Whiting of the Pahiatua Police Department began addressing him as sir almost immediately while allowing him to make a private call to Wellington in his office and putting on a kettle for tea whilst he waited for the low rumble in the next room to conclude.

"And what's your name, miss?" he asked as he handed Kate a cup of tea in a cracked Royal Doulton cup with a mismatched saucer.

She took a hesitant sip and told him her name.

"Oh. Not related to the Feilding Hardys, I suppose."

"Yes," she said, accepting the inevitable. "I am. I'm Sam Hardy's daughter if you must know."

"Ah." He stirred his tea and said nothing for a while and then asked, "How did you get mixed up in this business, Miss Hardy, if you don't mind me asking?"

She sighed deeply. How had she got mixed up in this business? Good question.

"It's a long story. I ran into the major on the way to my family farm, and I haven't been able to shake him off ever since. He keeps turning up like a bad penny."

They sat in silence, sipping their tea, until Harry returned from the other room.

"We're good. Captain Bates at the S.I.B. has dispatched a team to track down the woman from Massey College — Lina Meyer — and the man driving the Jeep, whoever he is. It shouldn't be difficult. Not many Jeeps out there, and I told them the number on the front. They'll get him."

She put down her cup.

"I'm sorry, Harry. With all the fuss, I forgot to mention that he went over a cliff in his Jeep on the Pahiatua Track. I saw it happen." She glanced at the sergeant, sipping his tea and pretending not to listen, his eyes wide and attentive. "The Jeep had a flat tire, and he couldn't steer it and went down a steep hill. He was stuck part way down, so I went down with a rope to…"

"You did what?" he snapped. "Kate, you're going to have to stop trying to rescue everyone. I'm grateful you came to rescue me, but really, go back to Wellington and stay out of this. You're going to get yourself killed."

He must have seen something change in her face because he leaned over and put his hand on hers. "I'd hate to see you get killed, Kate, because I care about you. I'll go with you back to Wellington today if you like. I'm heading there for a meeting with the head of S.I.B. to discuss our next steps. We'll be rounding up the members of the Eugenics Society, and you don't want to be part of that."

Sergeant Whiting perked up. "The Eugenics Society? Why will you be rounding up the members of the Eugenics Society?"

Harry thought for a minute, tapping his fingers on the table. "Do you have something to tell me about the Eugenics Society, sergeant?"

"Well, yes, I do. Miss Hardy just mentioned she was Sam Hardy's daughter, and I know his brother-in-law Hamlet Sorensen very well. He lives over by the camp. Did you know he was the founding member of the Eugenics Society? It's because of the boy. The boy that was born twenty or so years ago."

"What boy?" said Kate. "Hamlet doesn't have any children. I've known him my whole life, and I've never heard there was a son."

Harry held her hand firmly in both of his as if he suspected she was about to be told something she wouldn't want to hear. Sergeant Whiting was looking increasingly embarrassed. "There was a boy. He's still alive, I believe. He's a Mongol child, and he's in the lunatic asylum in Wellington. I'm sorry, we don't say that anymore, do we? He's in the Porirua Mental Hospital. Has been for most of his life."

Kate could hardly breathe. How did she not know about this? She stared at Sergeant Whiting, grappling with the new information.

"Is that why he started the Eugenics Society then? Because he had a son who was mentally handicapped? Is that why he's always down in Wellington?"

"I imagine so. Also, as I'm sure you know, he's friendly with the prime minister, Peter Fraser, and visits him."

"Is he? When he's in Wellington, he takes me out for tea," said Kate. "But I can't remember him mentioning the prime minister or saying he was meeting him. I thought it was because he was on one of the hospital boards. Are you sure he knows the prime minister?"

"I saw a photograph of him with Fraser in his study," said Harry.

"He's more of a friend to Mrs. Fraser, the prime minister's wife," said Sergeant Whiting. "She's a member of the Wellington Hospital Board, and she's also on the Mental Defectives Board and the Eugenics Board. That's why I doubt that your group is harboring spies if that's what you're thinking. The prime minister's wife would certainly not have any connection to a group that's protecting traitors. It's unthinkable."

Kate pulled her hand away from Harry and took the flier from her pocket. "Here's a list of the people in the Eugenics Society. Hamlet is on there, and Lina as well."

Harry scanned the names on the flier. "I don't see Lina's name here."

"The receptionist at Massey College said she was the secretary of the group. Is Professor Collins's name on the list? He denied belonging to that group, but I didn't believe him."

"Nope." Harry looked up at Kate. "Maybe there's another group, and the receptionist was confused."

Two groups? It seemed unlikely. She'd never heard of anyone being interested in Eugenics before. No one in her family mentioned it. Was the receptionist at Massey College part of a conspiracy? Was Lina? And what about Hamlet, her beloved uncle? If there was another group out there, maybe it had nothing to do with Eugenics.

"Where's Professor Collins now? Still at the internment camp? We should ask him if he belongs to a group that Lina belongs to."

"I'll give the camp a call. But asking him to tell us the name of a group of traitors he's part of might not be the best idea."

"Dr. Klein!" said Kate.

"What about him?"

"We could speak with him. He might have seen something. Lina was visiting someone in the special compound. I saw her wave in that direction when she was leaving. And Professor Collins was waiting to speak with Dr. Klein because he had a visitor. So I assumed the visitor was Lina, but I can't be sure. Maybe she was visiting someone else. Dr. Klein would have seen who it was."

"Right then. We'll have a session with the good doctor," said Harry. "See if he can tell us anything. After that, we'll pick up the Roadster at the farm and get my bike in Feilding. Then you can return to Wellington. Will your uncle stay at the farm until the farmhands are back in the cottage?"

"Yes," said Kate, feeling flat suddenly. Had he changed his mind about going to Wellington with her? If so, their time together had shortened drastically.

"And we can get together in Wellington while I'm there. Maybe go to one of the forces clubs for a decent meal and a dance. Do you like to dance?"

"I love dancing. Don't tell me you can dance?"

"I get by."

"It's a date." She smiled, relieved. "As long as it's not at the Allied Services Club. You heard about what happened there, did you? Back in April?"

"No. I wasn't in New Zealand in April. What happened?"

"Some American soldiers and our boys got into a fight about Māori soldiers being allowed into the club. The American shore patrol came along and knocked them out with batons and took them away. We don't do that here, separate the races, as you might have noticed."

He nodded. "Not the Allied Services Club, then. I'll find somewhere more classy."

Sergeant Whiting was looking at them with open disdain. Kate realized they'd been moving closer and closer together, their hands touching, and leaned back, trying not to show her satisfaction to either of the men.

"Are you going to the internment camp then?" asked the sergeant brusquely. "I need to write up my report."

Harry sprang to his feet. "Yes, sergeant. We're off. Thank you for all your help."

It seemed strange to return to the internment camp so soon after they'd escaped from it, but their reception was not the least bit like the earlier one, no more than an hour or so earlier. Major Perrett, the commandant, met them at the gate and apologized profusely to Harry for not knowing he'd been held captive in the infirmary.

"A nurse brought you in, and she had papers saying you had escaped from an asylum and needed to be kept here until the asylum guards came to collect you."

"What did she look like, this nurse?"

"Quite striking," said Major Perret. "Hair pulled back like this." He pulled his hair back from his forehead. "Very well made up, with red lipstick and long red nails. A little older than Miss Hardy, perhaps about ten years older. A grown woman."

"And wearing a camel coat?" asked Kate. The nurse had quite obviously been Lina. "Not a nurse's uniform?"

He nodded. "Yes, and she was very attractive," he said, as if wearing a camel coat had sealed the deal for him.

"How did she get me into the infirmary?" asked Harry. "I'm

not a lightweight, and I was unconscious. Did someone help her?"

"She asked the guard at the gate for assistance," said Major Perrett. "And I'm embarrassed to admit it, but we sent two guards to carry you in. You were completely out and smelled of alcohol. She said you'd gone straight to a bar after you escaped from the institution."

"Did she say how she managed to get me into her car?"

Major Perrett's lips tightened. "I had no reason to ask her. I say, major, we took her at her word because she had papers proving you were an inmate. And it wasn't as if she was trying to get you out of here. She was bringing you in. And you do look as if you have German ancestry, so this seemed to be the right place for you. Of course, once you came around, we would have realized you weren't an insane person."

Harry raised his eyebrows. "Really? You're able to diagnose insanity?"

Kate nudged Harry. "What we need to know is who was she visiting in the special compound when she was here earlier today."

"She didn't visit anyone in there," said Perret firmly. "She went to the infirmary for ten minutes, and then she left. If she waved to someone, it could have been a guard. One of the guards at the entrance to the special compound was rather friendly to her, but he may have been attracted by her appearance. Even the fact that she waved at someone as she left could have been simply her thanking someone who had helped her."

"You could be right," said Harry. Kate heard a tinge of doubt in his voice. "What we'll do is talk to Dr. Klein and then the guard. Is that okay with you?"

"Dr. Klein's English is not very good," said the commandant.

"I can find you a translator if you need one. We have someone local who speaks perfect German, and we bring her in to translate frequently because he has so many visitors. He's known internationally for his theories, you know."

"Miss Hardy speaks fluent German," said Harry. "That's why I brought her with me."

"Why did you tell him that?" asked Kate as they were escorted to the gate of the special compound. "I could read Dr. Klein a bedtime story in German, but not much more than that. And I wouldn't even understand what I was reading."

"Keeping my powder dry," said Harry. "No one expects Americans to speak another language. Hell, I don't even speak your language."

She laughed. "Kiwi, you mean? You should try understanding 'Strine. That's Australian if you're wondering. Don't worry, you'll get used to it. You'll even start speaking like us. When you go back to America, they'll all be asking you where you're from."

Dr. Klein was sitting on a wooden bench in the sunshine, bent over, scribbling in a notebook with the stub of a pencil. He reminded her of someone. Who was it? He wore a rumpled old tweed suit with a cardigan under the jacket, had deep grooves down either cheek and a bristly dark gray mustache. If she saw him in the street, she would immediately assume he was a professor of some sort.

That was who he looked like. Albert Einstein. Only younger.

Harry squatted in front of him and said, "*Guten tag, Herr Doktor.*"

He left his pencil poised above his notebook and glanced between Harry and Kate.

"What do you want?"

"Lina Meyer," said Harry.

"*Who? Ich kenne diese Frau nicht.*"

"Says he doesn't know her," Harry said to Kate.

"And I do not," said Dr. Klein.

"She was here earlier, and when she left, she waved goodbye to you," said Kate.

"*Nicht ich.*" he said. Not me.

He had understood her perfectly well. Wouldn't he need to understand and speak English if he was teaching at Massey College? Surely, they wouldn't hire someone, no matter how famous, who couldn't make himself understood by the students. Which made her wonder why he needed a translator.

"He mustn't have understood me. Perhaps he does need a translator, as the commandant suggested," she said to Harry, speaking as quickly as she could.

A look of annoyance crossed Dr. Klein's face.

Harry had remained crouched in front of the doctor. He glanced at Kate and then spoke again in rapid German. Kate understood the occasional word but was soon lost. She wandered away from them and studied the rest of the inhabitants of the special compound. They were all men and mostly middle-aged or older. They didn't look particularly dangerous, and she wondered what they had done to warrant putting them in here. Was it just that they were recent arrivals from Germany? Or had they done something since they had been interned?

They had passed two armed guards on the way into the compound, one of whom was Lina's friend, according to Major Perret, who gestured at the guard with his head and said, "This is the guard I mentioned."

The guard nodded at Harry and said, "Sir."

THE PAHIATUA POLICE STATION

"We need to talk," Harry had said. "I have some questions that need answers."

Shortly after Harry began speaking to the doctor, she saw the guard leaving the compound; he was replaced by a different guard.

Eventually, Harry stood up and stretched. He leaned forward and shook hands with the doctor, who smiled slightly and then returned to his notebook, a look of concentration on his face as he made notes about something.

"I'll tell you what he said later," he said to Kate. "I think we should return to Palmerston over the Pahiatua Track. I'd like to see the place where the Jeep went over."

"Are you feeling guilty?" asked Kate. "About the slashed tires, I mean."

He shrugged. "He decided to take that road. His tires would already have been soft. He should know how to take care of a Jeep if he's going to race around in it, especially over that treacherous road. Well, let's get the guard out of the way. Where is he? I thought he was at the entrance to the compound."

"Too late. He left already."

"Huh. Well, she probably flirted with him to get him to do what she wanted him to. I can't see that he'd know her."

"Are we off to the Pahiatua Track then? I must warn you, Uncle Joey's car will make hard work of it. You might have to get out and push, or I might even have to drive it backward uphill."

He grinned down at her. "We aren't in a hurry, are we?"

She felt herself blushing again.

"I suppose not."

17

The Chase

Harry needed a quiet place to tell Kate some awkward information: the translator who lived nearby and spoke perfect German was Helga Sorensen, Hamlet's wife, and Kate's aunt. She'd been coming to the camp for months and was the first person they called when they needed a German translator. It was almost her second home by the sound of it.

Dr. Klein had not told him that Helga was the translator. All he'd said was a German woman who lived within walking distance of the internment camp had been acting as a translator for him. He had been surprised when Harry asked if the translator was Helga Sorensen but agreed that it was.

Helga had been at the camp the night before the escape to translate for Dr. Klein, who was writing an academic treatise. She would copy his work into English so that he could submit it to an academic journal and would take it home and type it out for him. And she had invited him to her place for dinner, not for the first time, the night of the escape. Major Perret had denied her request several times but had finally agreed he could go if a guard went with him. He had, therefore, been at Hamlet's place on the night of the escape, looking over the manuscript and discussing it with Hamlet, who could understand German and speak a little.

He'd told Harry that he was looking forward to visiting Hamlet and his wife again. Did Harry know Hamlet Sorensen, he'd asked. What an excellent fellow, and very interested in Dr. Klein's subject matter. Helga had shown Hamlet the English version of the treatise.

Harry wasn't sure what to make of this information as it connected Dr. Klein to the prime minister himself indirectly. But how would Dr. Klein know about the connection in advance? And how would he know that internees would be moved to Pahiatua and kept in the local race course, which just happened to be next door to the Sorensen farm?

At best, it would be a lucky break if he was one of the conspirators, and as he was still in the camp, that seemed unlikely. He would not have even needed to climb the fence but would simply walk away from Hamlet's house. In some ways, the visit exonerated both Dr. Klein and Hamlet.

When asked what he was doing in the special compound, Dr. Klein had claimed he'd been put there for his protection as he'd been subject to an attack from 'certain people.' He refused to say who those people were but admitted that the camp was divided into factions, some political, some war-related. Germans had been tossed in with Poles and Slovaks, even some German Jews. And all of them stuck to their own.

Harry wanted to see the place where the Jeep had gone over the edge, partly to be sure in his mind that the driver could not have survived, but also to know that Kate hadn't risked her life trying to save someone who had no chance of surviving. She wasn't the soldier she thought she was, and he wondered what she would do if she was faced with a real enemy. He doubted she could handle real combat.

He'd fought with a lot of different men, but it was the first time he'd worked so closely with a woman. Was it always like this, split between wanting her assistance and wanting to take care of her? That was why women couldn't ever be soldiers. The men would always feel the need to protect them. Best leave women to do clerical work, farming, or even code-breaking. Free up the men for the battle.

Kate would not agree with him, of course. She'd say she'd climbed a fence and taken a hostage to save him and had also kept a shooter at bay with her grandfather's ancient rifle. All true, but the circumstances were exceptional.

Once they reached the spot on the Pahiatua Track where the Jeep had gone over, he could tell Kate what he had learned, giving him a chance to gauge her reaction with no one else around. Did she already suspect Hamlet and Helga, or would the information come as a complete surprise to her? He knew she was fond of Hamlet.

But as it turned out, they were not alone at the site of the wreck.

They chugged up to the spot, and Kate parked the car behind a police car. A constable stood guard beside the post from which Kate had lowered herself down towards the Jeep. The rope was still attached to it.

She smiled at the constable, who recognized her, and she went over to speak with him while Harry searched the hill for signs of life.

The Jeep was at the bottom of the slope, a good two hundred yards away, upside down and still smoldering. A fire engine sat near the farmhouse, and several firemen were attempting to douse the embers. More men — police from what he could tell this far away — were climbing the hill in a line. They could only be looking for a body. So they hadn't found him yet. And he wasn't in the Jeep, or they wouldn't be looking.

Kate returned, the rope dangling from her arm.

"They were wondering who this belonged to. I gave him a brief statement. I told him I happened to be passing, which is true."

"Did he say anything about a body?"

She shook her head. "Surely the driver must be dead. I don't know how anyone could have survived a fall like that. The Jeep flipped over several times. He'd be underneath it."

"The cops are looking for something on the hill."

"The rifle, maybe? I saw a rifle in the Jeep just before it fell."

"You didn't tell me that. Did you tell the constable?"

"They'd wonder why it mattered if I told them. He was going for it as he fell, so he probably knocked it out of the Jeep."

"What do you mean, going for it? Why was he going for it?"

"Well, I said he would go to prison for trying to shoot me, and he knew my name."

Harry shook his head and sighed. "Kate, Kate, Kate."

"At least we know for certain he was the person who shot at me," she said defensively.

"Let's take a walk and catch up with what we know, just to be sure I'm not missing anything else."

She walked along the edge of the drop, making him nervous. One wrong step and she'd be gone, but it didn't seem to worry her. It worried him. The thought of her falling down the hill before he could grab her scared the hell out of him.

She took the news about Hamlet and Helga calmly.

"I never liked Helga much. I'm sure if anything's going on with them, it's because of her, not him."

"Maybe she never got over having a Mongol child," he said. "That might be why she takes good care of Jens."

"She never goes down to Porirua to see him," said Kate. "Hamlet always comes to Wellington by himself."

"I'd guess she'd rather pretend he doesn't exist, but I guarantee it's eating away at her. Something sure is. I'm not ready to brand them as traitors or Dr. Klein. He came to New Zealand in nineteen thirty-eight. I don't know why he can't speak better English by now or why he even needs a translator, but some people don't have a knack for languages."

Kate sighed. "I'm sure Hamlet isn't a traitor, but I don't know about the other two. Is it possible that the Germans were prescient enough to plant Dr. Klein in New Zealand before the war because they guessed Americans would be here as a staging ground for war in the Pacific? We were always worried about what they were up to at home. But Germans, here?"

"You said your uncles fought in the First World War. The Germans would know New Zealand would side with Britain."

She nodded. "I suppose they would. There's something I haven't told you."

"Really? Could it possibly be something important?"

She smiled finally. "Not especially important. Just that I was born in England, in Walton-on-Thames. My mother was a nurse at the New Zealand hospital there, caring for wounded troops. My father was taken there when he was injured, and she nursed him. She came to New Zealand as a war bride in 1919. I was just a baby, so I can't remember coming here. She died of influenza soon after they arrived, the same thing that killed my grandfather."

"And your father has never remarried?"

She looked away from him, embarrassed. "He has a lady friend. She's still married to someone else."

"As long as we're confessing things," he said. "I wasn't born in America."

"Don't tell me. You were born in Germany, weren't you?"

He nodded. "During the First World War. After the war, my father sent his wife and parents to America because times were so hard. I was six when we moved, and my mother never learned English. That's why my German is so good."

"Is your father still alive?"

He shrugged. "I guess he is. If so, he's fighting for the Nazis. We lost touch years ago."

"And yet, here we are, strolling along a hillside together as if our families have never been at war with each other."

"We should get moving," he said. "We have to pick up your car and then fetch my motorcycle."

"One more thing I want to know," she said. "The man whose body we saw on the rocks near the Marine camp. Who was he? I know you recognized him, and you said he was in the internment camp, but who was he?"

"He was an Irishman," he said. "Young guy. He came here early in the war. He had two advantages. One was that some distant members of his family had belonged to the IRA, the Irish Republican Army, so we could pass him off as an enemy of England. The other advantage was that his mother was German, and he understood German well enough to eavesdrop on other internees. We put him in the camp on Somes Island and let him get to know people. He was a garrulous type and made friends easily."

She sniffed. "I thought that was who he was," she said.

What do you mean? Did you know him?"

"No. But I think I might know his family."

"Sorry."

They returned to the car in silence. She threw the rope onto the back and slid into the passenger seat.

"We'll be at the farm in under an hour," she said. "Feel free to lean back and have a nap. If I drive off the edge of the road, I'll tap you on the arm so you can brace yourself."

He laughed. "The way you drive, I think I'll sit bolt upright and hang on to my seat."

"Wait until I'm back in the Roadster," she said. "Then you'll have something to worry about."

"Do the cops stop you if you're speeding?"

"Not around here. They know who I am."

"Must be nice."

He leaned back on the battered leather seat and closed his eyes, just for a few minutes.

He woke when she tapped him on the arm, and he discovered that they were already at the farm.

"Wake up, sleepyhead. My car's here, and Uncle Joey is not, so we can head right over to get your bike in Feilding."

Feilding was another twenty minutes away, and she drove the distance at top speed, as threatened. At least the road was straight with no steep drops anywhere.

His bike had gone.

He thrashed through the bush, hoping someone had just moved it to a safer place or he'd forgotten where he left it, but he knew it had been taken. He could see where the ferns had been flattened as someone wheeled it away.

Kate was waiting for him in the Roadster, as he knew she

would be.

"Not there?"

"Nope."

"Here we go again. Where shall I take you this time? Back to Wellington?"

He rubbed his eyes, still feeling the after-effects of the drug.

"Maybe. But I should stop at Camp Russell and talk to the doctor. He'll have done an autopsy by now, and there might be something he can tell me."

"What was his name, the young man who was murdered?"

"Foster. Sean Foster."

The car was already moving, and it lurched forward abruptly as her leg jerked downwards. Her face had gone pale, and she looked as if she was about to cry. What the hell was that about?

He was afraid to ask. But getting emotional about someone she'd never met did show she didn't have the fortitude to be a soldier. She had guts, though. And she was a fearless driver.

She drove the Roadster through one small New Zealand town after another, the main streets lined with telegraph poles and cabbage trees, butcher shops, bakeries, low wooden hotels, majestic bank buildings made of wood, and general stores still with places to tie up horses. He felt almost as if he had returned to the old west. All the towns needed was a saloon with swinging doors and two men aiming revolvers at each other in the main street as tumbleweed floated by.

Soon, they were near the coast, with the wind coming off the ocean and moving the car from side to side. He was watching her as she drove, noticing how easily she handled the car, admiring her skill, when he noticed that she kept glancing in the side door mirror.

"What are you looking at? Are we being followed?."

"I keep seeing a motorcycle behind us. It's been back there for a while, not getting closer or falling back but going the same speed as we are. If I speed up, it keeps up with me. It looks like your motorcycle."

He spun round. The car was kicking up dust, but he could see the faint shape of a motorcycle a hundred yards behind them.

"How far are we from Camp Russell?"

"Thirty minutes."

"Is there a place coming up we can get off the main road and double back behind him?"

She thought for a minute, her eyes darting back and forth between the road and the mirror.

"There's a dirt track on the other side of the next bridge that would work."

"Right. Get off quickly, but wait to get back onto the road until you see the bike go by. Then, catch up to him from behind. If it's who I think it is, we'll drive him off the road."

They crossed a bridge, and she swung sharply to the left, causing him to lean over and grab her shoulder. She kept control until they had raced along the dusty track and back to the road just as the bike roared by.

"There he is. After him."

She drove as if she was trying to qualify for the Indy 500, narrowing the gap between the car and the bike quickly.

"That's my bike," he said, pointing. "See that mudguard? It's still bent from the crash."

"I'm glad you're sure. I'm going to bump into him. Hold on."

As she gained on him, the bike rider slammed on the brakes as he searched for them ahead. She dragged the Roadster to the right but couldn't avoid clipping him. The car spun around while she dragged at the wheel until they came to a stop facing the other way. She slumped over the wheel, breathing heavily.

"Oh my God. I thought we were both going to die."

"Are you okay? No injuries?"

"No. I'm fine. What happened to the man on your bike?"

"He's over by the tree. My bike's standing up, and he's on the ground beside it. He's moving, so we didn't kill him."

He jumped from the car. "Wait here. I'll get him."

The guard from the internment camp was slumped on the ground beside the bike, holding his arm.

"I dislocated my bloody arm," he said. "What the fuck were you doing?"

"Trying to get my bike back. Sit up, and I'll get your arm back in the socket."

The guard sat up, wincing in pain. Harry crouched down and pulled the limp arm down slowly, then twisted it around a fraction.

"What are you doing? That's not putting it back....aagh. Stop, stop, you're making it worse."

Harry released his grip on the guard's arm slightly and let it slide back to where it had been. He'd dislocated his arm once, and it had hurt like hell. Worse than childbirth, someone had said, although he couldn't imagine anything worse.

"Who sent you? Why were you following us?"

"No one sent ... ouch. What are you doing?"

"Not much yet. But I'll pull your arm out so far it'll never be right again unless you tell me who sent you after us."

Kate had come up behind him. "Do you have to hurt him, Harry? I'm sure he'll tell us if we ask nicely."

The guard was grunting in pain, his face contorted, unable to speak.

"Tell you what," said Harry. "I'll give you some names, and you can nod if you recognize any of them. That way, when they visit you in prison, you can deny that you said anything."

Harry let the arm hang loose again and sat back, waiting for a reply.

The guard nursed his arm and looked at Harry through hate-filled eyes.

"I'm not a traitor."

"Maybe not, but you're a thief," said Harry. "Alright, let's start with some names. Mr. and Mrs. Sorensen."

The guard shook his head. "Mrs. Sorensen translates stuff for Dr. Klein. That's all I know about her. I've never seen Mr. Sorensen."

"Okay then," said Harry. "What about Dr. Klein?"

"Dunno. I don't have anything to do with him. He works all the time, and people come and see him like he's a film star or something."

"Who told you to pick up the bike."

"Someone in the camp runs the whole thing. I just do as I'm told."

"You just follow orders, eh?"

Harry pushed the guard's head forward so his arm dangled down and gave the arm a quick tug. The guard gave a muffled scream and then stopped, an astonished look on his face.

"It stopped hurting."

"Right. Well, I'm going to tie you up and put you in the trunk of the car. Where's the nearest police station, Kate?"

"Paekākāriki, I think, But you have to pass Camp Russell to get there. You might as well go right to Camp Russell. They'll take him, won't they?"

THE CHASE

It felt good to be back on his bike, following Kate to the Marine Corps camp. Once they dropped off the guard and he called Captain Bates at S.I.B., he and Kate would return to Wellington, each driving a different vehicle.

That would probably be it for Kate. She was getting to be too much of a distraction for him. Time to go their separate ways. He had a faint twinge as he thought of not seeing her again. Was that really what he wanted? He could think about it later.

18

Back to Camp Russell

As she turned down the dirt road towards Camp Russell, Kate could see dozens of men in full Marine gear running up a long, steep hill in the distance. The search for the last body was over, and normal life had resumed. The guard opened the gate and gestured for her to enter. The sound of the internment camp guard thumping around in the boot of the Roadster had not stopped since they'd stuffed him in there, so she pointed back to the main road and mouthed, "I'm waiting for someone."

She backed the car off the road and waited for Harry to appear. He was following her on his damaged bike, the mudguard scraping against the tire, forcing him to drive much more carefully than normal.

After they had put the guard in the boot of the Roadster, he'd asked her to drive him back to Wellington.

"You're not getting rid of me yet," he said.

"I never thought I would," she said. "There always seems to be another reason we have to go somewhere together. You just watch. Something will happen at Camp Russell that sends us off on another wild goose chase. We're not going to Wellington for at least another day."

"If you say so," he said, grinning. "I think we're living in a movie. Tracy and Hepburn, that's who we are."

She had no idea who Tracy and Hepburn were but hoped they were young and attractive and destined to be together for a long time.

He puttered up on his Indian ten minutes later and flipped his card at the guard, who made a show of checking it out.

"She's with me," he said. "I need to see the doctor and the commandant. Did you find the missing man from the accident yet?"

The guard shook his head. "No, sir. We're not going to find him now. He'll have washed down the coast. The *U.S. American Legion* has returned to Wellington with the men who were rescued. The bodies are here and will be buried in a site of the next farm. We're back to normal now, Sir. We're even having a dance at the recreational hall on Saturday night."

"Some of us are back to normal," said Harry. "Do you mind if I leave my bike inside the gate somewhere? It needs to be repaired, but I don't have the time right now. And by the way, there's a prisoner in the trunk of the young lady's car. Could you get him out and keep him somewhere? He's a high-risk type, so make it somewhere secure."

The guard was unfazed. He opened the boot and pulled out the guard from the internment camp, accidentally using his injured arm.

"By the way," said Harry, "he dislocated his arm. He might need medical attention."

Camp Russell had come back to life. Young men in fatigues were everywhere, sitting outside the recreation hall smoking, kicking a ball around in an open area, and polishing boots in front of their tents. Outside the P.X., a long line snaked around to the building.

She parked the Roadster outside the commandant's office and asked, "Shall I come in, or would you rather I stayed outside?"

He glanced at the activity and raised his eyebrows.

"I don't think you'll last long out here on your own. Better come inside with me, but sit quietly if you can."

The commandant was in his office and bristling with new information.

"Captain Bates of S.I.B. called earlier. He said you'd be dropping by. As I'm sure you know, they're searching for a Jeep, and he gave me the number. It was one of ours that has been missing for a few days, so we were pleased to be able to inform him of that."

"Did he tell you where the Jeep is now?" asked Kate, unable to keep her mouth shut.

The commandant glanced at Harry, who shrugged and looked amused.

"Um, no, he didn't know. Have you seen it?"

"Several times," said Kate. "The first time I saw it was here. It was leaving as we came in. I don't know the number, but I know it was the same Jeep because I recognized the driver the next two times I saw him."

"So you saw him three times altogether?"

"Yes, the second time doesn't matter, but the third time, I saw him drive over the edge of the road and down a steep hill. The Jeep is at the bottom of the hill. It was on fire when we last saw it."

"And the man in it, you say it was also the same person? Is he dead?"

"We're not certain," said Harry. "But I can't see how he could have lived through the fall he took. Do you have any idea who the driver might be?"

"As it happens, I can help you with that as well. We're missing a Marine. We didn't realize he was gone for a day or two as we were so focused on making sure no one came in. But you saw him leave, did you, Miss Hardy?"

"Yes, I did. And he was in a Jeep. I believe it was the same Jeep."

"I'm assuming he took it," said the commandant. "If there's enough of the machine left at the bottom of the hill, we may be able to confirm the number By the way, his name is Captain Fisher, Captain Al Fisher."

"Hmm. Is that Fischer with a c?" asked Harry. "A German name?"

The commandant picked up a note from his desk. "His full name is Albrecht Fischer, last name spelled with a c. I suppose that suggests that he has German ancestry. Are you hinting that he was a mole planted in the Marines before the war?"

"Hard to know," said Harry. "He could have been turned after he enlisted. It's not up to me to find out. We have people who can do that. If you want to know where the Jeep is now and whether they found the dead Marine, you can call Sergeant Whiting at the Pahiatua Police Station."

The commandant wrote the name down on his note. "Whiting. Right. Got it. In Pahiatua, you say? How do you spell that?"

Kate spelled out the letters slowly and gave him a quick education on the pronunciation of Māori names. She didn't tell him that he could ring anyone in Pahiatua and ask for Sergeant Whiting, and they'd fetch him.

"Is the doctor around? I'd like to know if he found anything on the body during the autopsy," said Harry.

"I believe he did," said the commandant. "He found a piece of paper in the lad's throat. It had names on it, but he couldn't make them out as the paper was too wet. He was drying it last I spoke with him."

"Names?" asked Kate. "You mean he swallowed a list of names before he died?"

"Looks like it."

Harry stared into Kate's eyes. She stared back at him, reading his expression. He was wondering if she could handle someone from her family being on the list. She thought she could, but the knowledge that poor Sean Foster had swallowed a piece of paper, knowing he was about to die, shook her.

"I can take it."

"Are you sure?"

She nodded, and he squeezed her arm.

"Good girl. Let's go to the sick bay."

They left the commandant's office and walked through the camp to where the doctor had his office. Somehow, his arm had found its way over her shoulder and was draped there protectively. She tried to lean against him as if it was a normal thing. She knew he was worried about what they were about to find out, and the arm over her shoulders did make her feel more able to cope.

Now, if only Uncle Hamlet's name was not on the list, she could get through this.

"Here's the doctor's office," said Harry.

She turned to look up at him and discovered that he was looking down at her, and their faces were no more than a couple of inches apart.

Here goes, she thought. What have I got to lose? She went the extra inch and kissed him. He seemed to freeze for a minute and then began to return the kiss.

A minute of heaven, and then a voice said, "I'm not giving her the marriage blood test, son, just you. We don't do the women here. She'll have to see a local doctor."

They sprang apart. The doctor was frowning down at Harry from the steps of the surgery, his arms crossed.

"I was here a few days ago about the body on the beach," said Harry. "Major Wilhelm."

The doctor's face cleared. "Ah, yes, I remember. And the young lady was with you as well. Did the commandant tell you I discovered something in the victim's throat?"

Harry nodded. He seemed to have lost some of his assertiveness temporarily.

"Well then, come along inside, and I'll show you the list. I have it sitting under a radiant heat lamp. It's more or less dry now. The names are more or less legible."

Harry waited for Kate to climb the steps first, and she did so, feeling his eyes boring into her back.

A heat lamp sat on his office desk, glowing above a piece of paper on top of an old medical book.

"It's not quite dry yet, so don't touch it," said the doctor.

Harry bent over close to the list of names, stared at them for several minutes, and then glanced up at Kate.

"Hamlet isn't on the list," he said. "But Helga's name is here, I'm sorry to say. A couple of men from the internment camp, I'd guess. Do you know a man by the name of Dieter Schmidt?"

"He's the man from the Feilding race course I told you about. He can't be on the list. He's Jewish."

"Are you sure about that?"

"Not really. He said he was a conscientious objector because he didn't want to fight his cousins who were still in Germany."

"Hmm. Could be a Quaker." Harry continued to study the list. "Albrecht Fischer. He's there." He bent closer and squinted at the paper. "Wait a minute. Dr. Klein's name is here."

He straightened up and stared at Kate. "He had me fooled. I was sure he was just a mild-mannered scientist. Foster has drawn a double line under his name as well. That must mean something."

"He could be the leader ... oh no!"

"What?"

"He's having dinner tonight with Hamlet and Helga. And he knows we're on to them because we told him."

"We'd better get over to Phiatua," said Harry. "Thank you, doctor. Could you call Captain Bates at S.I.B. and let him know who's on this list? Your exchange will have the number. I called them before. Tell him we're on the way to the Sorensen farm next to the internment camp in Pahiatua. Have him send back up."

They hurried out to the car without saying anything more.

"We're going to need petrol before we leave. I'm almost out," Kate said as she started the engine.

"Damn. Over there beside the recreation hall. We'll get as much as we can and take a spare can in the trunk."

She drove over to a military-style petrol station and stopped beside a pump. Lots of petrol, by the look of it, on top of all the silk stockings and chocolates. They lived like kings, these Americans. Harry jumped out and grabbed the handle of the pump. She watched as he filled the tank and a spare can and flashed his card at the attendant. No money changed hands.

"Right. Let's go. How far is it to Pahiatua? About seventy-five miles?"

"More like eighty. We'll have to go over the Pahiatua Track because it's the shortest route, so it'll take at least two hours."

She heard him sigh. Trapped with her for two hours, the sigh said. They had plenty to discuss, but nothing he would want to talk about right now. She wasn't going to let him off that easily, however.

"What was the doctor talking about when he said he'd give you a marriage blood test, but not me? What would he be testing for?"

"Syphilis," he said abruptly. "In the States, you need to show you're not harboring communicable syphilis before they let you have a marriage license."

"Just as well we don't need one then," she said airily, hoping she didn't sound like she was afraid she would test positive.

He grunted in reply and stared out at the road. She didn't care. He could behave any way he wanted. She had something to remember now, and she knew she wasn't the only one.

More than an hour had passed, and they flew past the back of Massey College towards the entrance to the Pahiatua Track. Harry spoke for the first time since they'd left the Marine camp.

"We'll have to work out how this group interconnects."

"Through the internment camp, don't you think?"

"I guess. Dr. Klein could have recruited all the members from inside the camp. He met Helga there, we know that."

"Perhaps it was the other way round. Helga could have been the key person in the group and recruited everyone. I can imagine the Nazis seeding women around the world by marrying them off. Hamlet was never very successful with women. The Germans would have seen him coming when he was buying breeding horses."

"Yeah. Maybe. Then you've got a US Marine from the other side of the ranges and a woman — Lina, I'm talking about — who would have known Dr. Klein through Massey College. What's her job there, by the way?"

"I never actually asked. I saw her at the reception desk, and Professor Collins knew her when I went around the back and said she'd sent me to him."

"What about Professor Collins himself? He's not on the list. But he seems in the thick of things."

"He's a nasty piece of work, but I don't think he's one of them."

Harry put his arms behind his head, stretched out his elbows, and yawned.

"Are you tired?"

"I still feel like I'm tied to that cot. I need to get out and move around."

"We're almost there. Thirty minutes, and then you can run around the farm. I'm sorry Hamlet doesn't have any horses. I want to show you how to ride."

"One of these days," he said. "Does Hamlet have some spare bedrooms? I don't think I can go much longer before I get some rest."

"He has four bedrooms. Hamlet and Helga don't share one, so there are two spare rooms. One's a bit small, but I can sleep in that one. I always used to when I was a girl."

She could feel the word bedroom hanging between them like an apparition.

Finally, they were down on the plains and headed toward Hamlet's farm.

"What should we do when we get there?" she asked. "Sneak

up on them, or just walk in the front door as if nothing was wrong? Normally, I wouldn't knock."

"We should approach carefully," said Harry. "Even if they're all sitting at the table enjoying dinner, we might set him off. Them, I mean."

"How about I go in at the front, and you check everything out first?"

"Sounds good. I'm going to give you the sidearm. This is official business for me, and I want you to feel safe. No one will have a gun in there."

They pulled up in front of the farmhouse. No sign of Hamlet's car, but that didn't mean he wasn't home. Harry took off around to the back, and she watched him go, giving him time to get to check the place out. Then she raised her fist and knocked briskly on the door, a smile ready for Uncle Hamlet. He would be surprised that she had knocked, but that didn't matter.

A long silence, and then the door cracked open. An unsmiling Hamlet peered out.

"We don't want any today, thank you," he said loudly. "Please leave."

She could see a smear of blood on his shirt; his left eye was swollen.

She pushed past him and into the hallway. How dare they do that to her beloved uncle?

"Help is here, Uncle Hamlet."

Then, she wished she had not put the gun back in the holster.

Lina was standing behind Hamlet, a knife held against Professor Collins's neck.

19

Pursuing the Traitors

Lina backed slowly towards the sitting room at the front of the house, one arm around Professor Collins' neck, the blade dug into the professor's neck. Professor Collins's eyes were wide with fright, and he waved his hands at Kate.

"Please. Just leave."

Lina pushed the knife in a little further. It was a knife from a set Hamlet had purchased in Germany and kept well-sharpened.

"Are you alone?"

"Of course I am. I came to see my uncle. What have you done to him?"

"Get in here and sit down. You too, Sorensen. If either of you move, I'll slit Professor Collins's throat."

"Go ahead," said Kate. She sat on the sofa, tucking back her coat to ensure her hand landed near the gun. "What do I care if you slit his throat? He's a nasty man anyway."

Hamlet had tottered in after them. He sat down next to Kate and clutched at her arm.

"Don't say that, Katie. It's beneath you. You know you don't want her to kill an innocent man."

Beneath her? If only you knew, she thought. Her hand was now in contact with the gun, and she started to ease it out with her fingers. The last part would be difficult as Hamlet was in the way. She had to find a way to move him over.

"What happened, Uncle Ham? I thought Dr. Klein would be here. I came to say hello to him. Did he leave?"

He turned to her and nodded, his eyes welling with tears, freeing her arm slightly.

"They shot Jens, Katie. They shot my dear brother, who never harmed anyone. Dr. Klein knew about the old pistol I kept in my office; it was my brother Paul's old weapon. After he died in Gallipoli, the Army..."

"Enough of your goddamn history lesson," said Lina sharply. "I need her car. Give me the car keys."

"They're in the car," said Kate. "You won't get far. We'll have the police after you as soon you leave."

"Good luck with that. I cut the telephone line. I'll be well gone by the time you make it to the police station."

"What about me?" asked Collins. He leaned forward as if trying to free himself. "Are you taking me with you or leaving me here?"

He didn't sound quite scared enough, Kate realized. And his question could be interpreted both ways. Did he want to go with her?

"You're in on this, aren't you?" she said to him. "This is all a charade. Cut his throat, Lina. Go on. Do it."

"No need," she said smoothly. "Once we get outside, I'll knock him out and leave him on the ground."

"With a knife? You'll knock him out with a carving knife?"

The gun was in Kate's hand finally, and her finger hovered

above the trigger. She rose slowly and brought it around in front of her.

"Alright then. If he's not with you, you won't mind stabbing him. Go ahead and do it. If you don't, I'll shoot him in the thigh."

"Please don't do that, Katie," said Hamlet. "I can't stand to see anyone else shot. Not after what they did to Jens."

She hadn't paid attention earlier. "What happened to Jens?"

"He heard the fuss, and he got his old uniform on and came charging in. Dr. Klein grabbed the gun from the case and shot him. I had no idea it was loaded. Poor Jens didn't know what was going on. He thought he was going over the ridge to attack the Turks, and next thing, he was shot in the chest. He died in my arms."

Kate's whole body shook. "Oh, no. Poor Jens."

Lina gave Dr. Collins a shove. He banged against Kate, and together, they fell in a heap on the couch. The gun flew from her hands, and Lina scooped it up and pointed it at Kate.

"That's better. Come on, Bert. Let's get the hell out of here."

Professor Collins grabbed the knife and backed after her, grinning broadly.

Kate covered Hamlet with her body, afraid Lina would take one last shot. It was up to Harry now. She'd given him plenty of time.

In the hallway, her hand on the doorknob, Lina grunted suddenly and fell across the opening to the sitting room. Professor Collins tripped over her fallen body and fell against the wall, banging his head hard against the door frame on his way down.

"There you go," said Harry. He peered around the doorway. "A perfect strike. I think I get ten points for that one."

He put down the Bavarian crystal decanter he had used on Lina's head, picked up the knife and gun from the floor, stepped across the bodies, and flung open the front door.

"Come on in, gentlemen."

Kate put her arm around Hamlet as the room filled with men dressed in dark green utility uniforms. "The Marines are here," she said to Hamlet. "We're safe."

He leaned against her and sobbed.

"Oh, Katie, you've turned into your grandfather. I feel like such a fool that I couldn't save Jens. Mette will be so unhappy with me."

Harry perched on the arm of the couch next to Hamlet and looked past him at Kate. "Your grandfather, eh? I guess you're more of a warrior than I realized."

Kate blushed. Hamlet had not meant it as a compliment, but Harry had.

"I do my best."

"Did you learn anything we didn't know?" he asked. "Apart from Professor Collins belonging on Foster's list?"

Kate watched the Marines scoop up Lina by the arms and legs and haul her out the door. She was struggling uselessly, and it felt wonderful. Professor Collins would be next, and that would feel even better.

"Not much. Can you tell us where they're going, Uncle Ham? Did Helga say anything?"

"They're going to Castlepoint," said Hamlet. "Helga and Dr. Klein. I understand someone is picking them up tonight and taking them somewhere, maybe by sea, to Australia. Katie, I think she always knew she would do something like this from the minute I met her in Bohemia. She was always a traitor."

"How long since they left?" asked Harry.

"An hour, forty-five minutes. They took my car, a dark green La Salle Touring Sedan with four doors. The only one in New Zealand. It was stupid of them to have taken such a noticeable car, but they've done well so far, and they can't imagine not succeeding at this point."

"Is Castlepoint a port? Could a small ship land there without anyone noticing?"

"I've never been there," said Kate. "It is a village with a port, and there's a lighthouse, I know that. Sailing ships used to go there back in Granny's day, but I don't think they docked."

"Great. Our boys will catch them. I'm going with them, Kate. Wait here with Hamlet until I get back."

She jumped up. "No, Harry. I'm coming too. I'll follow in my car. I can't not be in at the end after all we've been through."

The leader of the Marines, a tall, distinguished man with crinkly eyes and tanned skin, had opened an ordinance map on the mantel and was tracing the way to Castlepoint.

"You won't be able to drive across the country in that Roadster outside, ma'am. I'll leave a medic with the elderly gentleman, and you can ride with me. Can you read a map?"

"I think so," she said. "I'm familiar with the land on this side of the ranges, so that will be useful."

"And you know the car we're chasing. Good. Major Wilhelm, you can hitch a ride in one of the other vehicles."

Harry frowned at the Marine and nodded. She waited for him to take charge, but for once, he didn't. The distinguished Marine must be at least a colonel.

They raced overland towards Castlepoint, six US Marine Jeeps spread out over the countryside carrying ten Marines, Harry and Kate. Colonel Smithson led the charge, and Kate half-expected to see a fox darting in front of them. She wanted to call out 'Tallyho!' but instead studied the map and directed the colonel toward the coast.

It was already dusk when they had left Hamlet at the farm; the medic had given him a shot in the arm of something strong, and he was snoring in his room when Sergeant Whiting arrived, shocked to see Jens lying dead on the floor of Hamlet's study.

"I'm sorry about your uncle," he said to Kate. "He didn't deserve this. I'll take care of his body, don't worry."

The traitors had a good hour and a half start by then, but the distance to Castlepoint was shortened dramatically by the Marines' route. Nothing got in their way. They'd been practicing for an assault like this for months.

The moon was up, and it was a clear night when they approached the coast, driving on the road down a steep incline. They could see the water stretched out before them, with a point jutting out into the ocean, Castlepoint, with the beam from the lighthouse moving slowly back and forth. On either side of the point lay sandy beaches, one blocked by a reef.

"There's the car," said Kate. "Down there on the beach road, about halfway along."

The colonel slowed the Jeep, waited for the other five to catch up, and then snapped out his orders.

"The vehicle is parked on the beach road to the north of the point. You three cover the north beach, one at each end of the road and one on the beach. Captain, cover the beach to the south of the lighthouse in case the car has been left as a decoy. Major Wilhelm, come with me to the lighthouse."

"Me too?" asked Kate.

"Of course. I hope you're not afraid of heights."

"She's not afraid of anything," said Harry.

"How about you, major? Nervous about heights?"

"Only when I'm worrying about someone else falling to her death."

The colonel looked thoughtfully at Kate and then at Harry, a faint smile on his lips.

"Understood."

The next part happened quickly. As she sprinted up the steep path overlooking the rocks to the base of the lighthouse, followed by Harry and the colonel, the Marines stormed the beaches on either side of the lighthouse.

The lighthouse sat on a narrow, flat area with steep drops on all sides. To the north, a grassy area jutted several feet higher. Kate scrambled up the slope.

"I can see everything from up here, Harry. Come and look."

"Keep away from the edge, Kate, for God's sake," said Harry. "It's bloody dangerous, and I can see everything just fine from back here."

"It's a much better view from up here. Come on up."

He edged up and stood next to her. She saw him look down towards the beach, his lips tight. Despite what he'd said, he was nervous. She slid her hand into his and leaned against him. "It's cold up here. Can you see them?"

"Yeah. It's a good view, you're right."

"They're running along the beach," said the colonel, who had followed Harry up the slope. "I can see their flashlight moving. They were trying to signal someone. There goes a Jeep after them. I wonder who they were signaling? Do you see a boat out there?"

Kate stared out at the beach but could see only blackness. Then, the light above them swept over the sand and she saw the two traitors hemmed in between two jeeps. Men with guns sprang out and surrounded them. A sense of relief washed over her.

"Got them."

"Let's go back and shelter beside the lighthouse," said Harry. He took Kate's arm in a firm grip. "It's bloody freezing up here."

Behind them, the colonel swore loudly.

"Look out to sea. Sweet Jesus, I wish I had some damned artillery up here. Christ, I'd give my left nut..."

Fifty yards out to sea, a dark shape had risen from the depths, water streaming from its hull like a deadly sea creature come to kill them all. A periscope rose slowly from the conning tower, and a Cyclopean eye surveyed the shore. Colonel Smithson had lost all his demeanor and was leaping around, waving his fists at the enemy submarine, ignoring the danger of the slope.

"You bastards. You're lucky the US Navy isn't here, you'd all be dead. I hope you hit one of your own damned land mines."

The eye withdrew slowly as the periscope was lowered, and the black hull slid slowly back from whence it had come, leaving a boiling maelstrom on the surface of the water.

The colonel turned to Harry. He was breathing heavily.

"Where the hell would it have come from? Was it German or Japanese? Could you tell?"

"It was a U 862," said Harry. "A U Boat, from the Dutch East Indies, I'd guess. It's a long way from home, though."

"Better alert the New Zealand Navy," said the colonel, who had returned to his normal calm self. "It could do some damage in these waters. Who do we know at the top of the food chain so we don't have to go through all the usual channels?"

Harry glanced at Kate, one eyebrow raised. She nodded. This

would be the right time to invoke her family connections.

"My father is the Chairman of the Special War Cabinet. Get me to a telephone, and I'll ring him and pass the phone to you."

"That's very convenient," said the colonel. "We can link cut into a telephone line to save time. There must be a line, even in a small town like this."

Fifteen minutes later, Kate found herself standing on the back of a Jeep beside a telephone pole, clutching a telephone headset connected to a line, informing her father that a submarine had been spotted in the waters off Castlepoint and that she was going to pass the telephone to Colonel Smithson of the U.S. Marines who would give him the details.

"Before you do that, tell me what the hell you've been up to, Kate. Joey rang and said my car was in a ditch, and someone had been shot at the farm, but not to worry, he'd got you a weapon. And something about an American Marine. I thought I told you to stay away from the Americans."

"Sorry, Dad. I'll explain everything later. But for now, here's Colonel Smithson."

She jumped off the Jeep, refusing several offers of help, and grinned at Harry.

"What next?"

"We're off back to Camp Russell," said the colonel. "Can we drop you off on the way?"

"Pahiatua," said Harry. "At Hamlet Sorensen's place. I don't think we can take much more than that. We've had one hell of a day."

It was well past midnight when they finally made it to Hamlet's farmhouse. This time, they didn't take the overland route but drove on the road in a convoy, traveling at top speed. Because the road was relatively smooth, Kate had dozed well before they arrived in Pahiatua. She woke up when the Jeep stopped suddenly and wondered where she was. Harry was standing beside her.

"We're here, Kate," he said. "There's a guard outside, and Hamlet is asleep."

"Thank you for all your help, Miss Hardy," said Colonel Smithson. "Major Wilhelm, the Chairman of the Special Cabinet, asked me to tell you he'd like to meet with you in the next day or two."

Harry nodded. He was almost asleep on his feet, and Kate wondered if he realized that he had just agreed to meet with her father. Why would her father want to meet Harry? He had something in mind, and she was afraid it was not something she would be happy about. Why did he want her to stay away from Americans? All Americans, or just Harry?

The house was dark, and they found their way into the sitting room and collapsed on the couch. "I don't think I've been this tired in my entire life," Harry said. He pressed the heels of his hands into his eyes. "Where are we sleeping? Is there a room each?"

She was at another turning point, and she'd known since they left Castlepoint what she would say. Her father was going to separate them, and she was determined to make it difficult for him.

"Let's take the room with the double bed. The other room is much too uncomfortable."

He moved his hands away from his eyes. "Are you sure?"

She nodded. "Stay here and close your eyes for a minute. I'll make up the bed and find you something to wear. I won't be long."

It took her less than ten minutes to put fresh sheets on the bed, lay out a pair of Hamlet's pajamas that would be too short but would do, and find a nice blue silk nightdress in Helga's room that looked like it had never been worn.

Then she patted the bedspread to remove the last wrinkle and returned to the sitting room.

Harry was stretched out on the couch, fast asleep.

She was tempted to pinch his arm or to put a cold washcloth on his face, but instead, she returned to the bedroom, found two blankets, and draped one of them over him. They'd had a long, difficult day, and they were both tired. She sat on a cushion on the floor beside him, wrapped herself in the other blanket, and leaned against the couch. Maybe he would wake up during the night. She wanted to make sure that if he did, he wouldn't just go back to sleep.

20

The Man in the Jeep

He awoke to the smell of coffee brewing, and for a minute, he thought he was back in Hawaii. The bed next to him was empty but still warm. Kate hadn't been up for long. He lay on his back, thinking about what had happened in the night. Was he happy about it? He thought so. Did he want more? Definitely.

Having made his decision, he got out of bed and pulled on his clothes. Time to face Kate and see what she thought about the situation.

Kate was in the kitchen talking to Hamlet Sorensen, leaning against the kitchen counter beside a drip coffee maker, both of them clutching empty mugs as the coffee dripped slowly into the carafe.

"Breakfast is almost ready," she said. "As soon as the coffee is through, Hamlet will make us toast with Marmite. We stocked up on it before the war — enough to last us until the end of 1945. No eggs, I'm sorry. Your lot gets them all."

A small jar with a yellow lid, filled with a dark brown substance, sat beside the toaster. Marmite, he saw on the red and white label. He had a feeling he wouldn't like it, but he would eat it anyway and wash it down with coffee. Couldn't go wrong with coffee.

He squeezed Kate's shoulder and sat down at the table beside Hamlet. She smiled slightly, came over, wrapped her arms around his neck, and kissed the top of his head.

"You'll hate Marmite," she said. "But you're going to have to get used to it because our troops get the butter, and yours get the cheese and milk. Marmite is good for you; they're feeding it to men in the POW camps to keep them healthy."

"I'm sure I'll like it. Has everyone else left?"

Hamlet sighed loudly. He was dressed in a suit, his hair smoothed back, his face clean-shaven. He put the coffee pot and three mugs on the table.

"The guard and the medic left twenty minutes ago. They claim we're safe now and that you'll take care of us if anything happens."

He poured himself a coffee and took a sip.

"Are you all right, Hamlet? You had a tough day yesterday."

"I'm quite well, thank you. I'm still in shock about my wife. About Helga. I knew she wasn't happy, but I didn't realize how bad things were. Of course, the situation with the boy didn't help. She couldn't stand seeing him, and I always went to visit him by myself."

Harry refrained from mentioning that Helga had probably been a plant from the start. Hamlet had enough on his plate.

"She was recruited by Dr. Klein," said Kate. She glanced at Harry, and he knew she wanted him to go with that story. "That's what I think."

"What will happen to them now?" asked Hamlet. "Her and Dr. Klein? Prison?"

"Detained until the end of the war," said Harry. "And then

repatriated to Germany. Unless the Axis powers win, of course, in that case, we might all be part of Asia."

"Don't even think that, Harry," said Kate. "The Germans and Japanese can't win this war. It's unthinkable."

He shrugged. "I hope not. But being on the right side doesn't mean we'll win."

"I'd like you to take care of the boy when I'm gone, Kate," said Hamlet. "I've set up a trust fund for him for when I die. I named you as the trustee."

"I'd be happy to do that, Uncle Ham, but you still have a long life ahead of you."

"A suppose I do," he said. He looked at Harry thoughtfully and then back at Kate. "But I wanted to make sure you knew about it in case you were thinking about leaving New Zealand for some reason. After the war, you know."

"What about the group you started?" asked Harry. "The Eugenics group. Are they connected to the spy ring, or is there another group somewhere?"

"No one in my group is a spy," said Hamlet firmly. "Other than Helga, of course. But she joined the group reluctantly and wouldn't attend meetings. And Professor Collins, of course, but he was there to find recruits. I'm not sure what they were planning to do. I guess we'll never know. Dr. Klein won't tell them anything."

"Someone must have an idea," said Harry. "All I was told was that a fifth column was forming, and they needed to find the epicenter. Then, when Foster was murdered, I knew we were on to something, but I didn't know what. I still don't know why he was on Kapiti Coast. He must have thought he was meeting someone. Me, maybe. But he met Al Fischer instead. The man in the Jeep who died on the Pahiatua Track."

"I've been thinking, Harry," said Kate. "No one has found his body, and the colonel told me it's possible he survived. We should check the area at the bottom of the hill ourselves. That farmhouse, for example. What if he's hiding in the barn or somewhere?"

"Wouldn't your police have checked the farmhouse?"

"Maybe. But they were searching the slope, not the bottom of the hill, so they were expecting to find a body."

"I guess. What do you want to do about it?"

"I think we should go to the farmhouse and check it out."

He put his hand over hers. "You know you're incorrigible, don't you?"

"She always was," said Hamlet. "Granny says she goes at life like a bull at a gate."

Harry grinned. It was not the most flattering image of Kate, but she did embrace life. He'd discovered that himself. "She knows what she wants," he said.

He expected Kate to blush, but it was Hamlet's face that slowly turned red. Hamlet was onto them. Was that why he was worrying about Kate leaving New Zealand? He thought Harry would take her away. He should be worried about that.

Kate pulled the Roadster up in front of the farmhouse beside an old truck. The morning sun was glinting off the windows at the front of the house. Nothing was left of the Jeep, but behind the farmhouse in the spot where it had ended its fall, a dark scar was burned onto the grass. No way he was alive, Harry thought. But it wouldn't hurt to have a quick look and ask the farmer if he'd seen a wounded Marine.

"Should we go right to the front door?" asked Kate. "Or shall we do the thing where I go to the front door, and you go around the back?"

"That's a thing?" He asked. He ran his fingertips along the inside of his lips, trying to get the taste of Marmite out of his mouth. Even the extra strong coffee hadn't helped wash it away. He'd rather be dropped back onto Guadalcanal from a helicopter than eat Marmite ever again. Thank God he wasn't a prisoner of war. He'd starve to death.

"I think we should go to the front door together," she said. "I'll talk so they don't realize you're an American."

"Alright," he said. "I'll stand there like your big dumb brother, and you do all the talking."

"You seem very jolly today."

"I am jolly," he said. "I had an excellent sleep last night."

This time, she blushed. "It was nice, wasn't it?"

"Let's go knock on the door. Nothing's going to happen, you know. He was either killed, or he survived and took off somewhere, which I doubt. He's not there. The police would have found him."

She knocked sharply on the door. After several minutes, the door opened a crack, and a woman in a flowery apron and pin curls held in place by a scarf looked out. She looked from Kate to Harry suspiciously.

"Can I help you?"

Kate leaned towards her, smiling brightly.

"Good morning, miss. I'm from the *Dominion*, the Wellington newspaper. I was wondering if you saw the accident yesterday, the Jeep that came down the hill. I just need a little quote. I'll put your name in the paper if you like."

Flowery apron's eyes narrowed. "I have nothing to say," she said. She slammed the door, surprised to find it wouldn't close because Harry's foot was in the way.

"Are you sure?" he said.

She turned and shrieked to someone behind her, "Davy, Davy, there's someone at the door asking about the Jeep. I think it's an American."

Harry had his hands flat against the door now, holding it open. A man came stamping down the hallway clutching a .22 calibre Winchester Model 52. Old and probably illegal, but the farmer had made a good choice. He'd probably stolen it when he was demobbed after the First World War.

"What do you want?" he said "Are you from the army?"

"Not your army," said Harry. He might as well be honest. "I'm a US Marine."

The man's face lost all its color. He lowered the rifle in Harry's direction. "Get the hell out of here, or I'll shoot you in the guts."

"We're here looking for the other US Marine," said Kate. "The one who was in the Jeep. He's a friend of Major…"

"He told me you might be here looking for him," said the man. "Fucking Marines. Can't leave a man in peace just because he doesn't want to fight."

Harry glanced at Kate. "Is that what he told you? It isn't true, you know."

"And he said you'd lie," said the man. "He even described you. He said you were chasing him when he went off the cliff. He could have died."

Harry took a deep breath. "He's not an AWOL Marine if that's what you believe. He's a German spy who was embedded in the American military, and he killed someone. Someone I knew."

"I don't believe you."

He slammed the door shut before Harry could stop him. Almost immediately, Harry heard a brief struggle followed by a grunt and then the familiar sound of a bolt being pulled back. He threw Kate to one side, landing on top of her, just as a gunshot blasted a hole in the door.

He sprang back up and hoisted her onto her feet.

"Run, Kate. Go along the road. And don't stop."

"I'm not leaving you..."

"Run," he roared at her. "For God's sake, Kate."

She backed away a couple of steps, then sprinted towards the car.

The car wouldn't provide shelter. "Along the road. Fast. Get to a telephone."

If he held off the killer long enough, she could get away and find help. Too late to tell her to call the Pahiatua police, but she'd think of them.

The door was hanging in tatters. He kicked it open. The woman in the apron screamed as chunks of wood from the door hit her in the face. She was pressed against the wall; her husband had retreated to the sitting room and was clutching the door jamb, blood pouring from his nose.

"I'm sorry. I didn't know..."

"Where is he?"

"He ran out the back," said the woman. "He took Bob's gun. And he's ruined our door. He almost hit me with that shot. It went right past my ear."

Harry pushed past them and went to the back of the house. The kitchen door was wide open, swinging back and forth on its hinges. A loaf of bread with a bread knife beside it sat on the counter. He picked up the knife and examined the door. Had the shooter gone out, or was he still in the house? He took a chance and went out the kitchen door at a run, flung himself on the ground, and rolled over. A shot blasted the kitchen window, shattering it.

Two things then. He'd gone outside, and he was a bad shot. If he couldn't hit his target with the Model 52, he couldn't shoot.

The barn was to Harry's right. The shooter hadn't had time to get there and aim his rifle. He'd gone for the slope, probably hoping for a height advantage.

A few yards away, an ancient tree drooped over the back garden. He crawled behind it and waited. Another shot hit the kitchen, this time the door. The shooter had not attended the course where he was told to shoot where the person was going, not where they'd come from. How had he made it in the Marine Corps? Did he have other skills?

He peered cautiously around the tree and saw the barrel of the gun above a ridge, just a quick glimpse, and then it was pulled away. The barn. He could go around that and up the hill behind it. The shooter would need to put his head up and watch where Harry was going, which he wouldn't. He didn't know that Harry wasn't armed, other than with a bread knife.

Harry came from behind the tree and sprinted to the cover of the barn. No shots fired. Was he out of rounds, or was he conserving what he had? Maybe three more? He'd grabbed the weapon from the farmer, so it was unlikely he'd have a spare magazine. And the farmer wouldn't spring for a ten-round magazine.

He went up the hill on his belly, keeping an eye on the spot where he'd last seen the shooter. He was level with the rise, about twenty yards to the right, when Fischer appeared above him, rising from the grass, his rifle pointing at Harry.

"Got you, you bastard."

Harry didn't wait for him to gloat some more but flung himself forward and grabbed him by the ankles. He caught him by surprise, and they tumbled down the hill together. The rifle flew away, and so did the bread knife. Fair exchange, Harry. Harry was sure he could take the guy in hand-to-hand combat, no problem.

They faced each other at the bottom of the slope, a few feet from where the jeep had landed. This time, Fischer attacked first, launching himself feet first at Harry's chest. Harry sidestepped but caught a boot against his shoulder. So not a shooter, but a Jujitsu expert. Good to know.

He bent down and waited for Fischer's next move. Fischer did a kind of twirl and came at Harry with his feet again. Harry sidestepped the feet but found himself in a headlock. He tried to flip Fischer over, but Fischer was ahead of him, twisting Harry's arm behind his back. He lowered himself and picked up the bread knife.

"What were you going to do with this, asshole? Slice me up? It'll work on your throat, I bet."

"No use killing me," said Harry. "You won't get away. Why not take your chances with the Military Police? Your word against mine."

"I don't think so. And I'll enjoy..."

"Put down the knife," said Kate. She had appeared from nowhere and had the rifle pointed at them.

Fischer pulled Harry closer and pressed the knife against his neck.

"What are you gonna do, girly? Shoot me through your boyfriend? Do you even know if the gun is loaded?"

Kate pulled the bolt and stared down the barrel, one eye closed.

"Don't kill him, Kate, for God's sake," said Harry.

"She won't get me without hitting you," said Fischer. "She's a girl. She has no idea..."

Harry heard the bullet whiz past him. Fischer dropped the knife and bent over, blood gushing between his fingers. "You bitch. You shot my ear off."

"Put your hands up and step away from Major Wilhelm," said Kate. "Or I'll shoot the other ear off."

He complied, sneering. "It's your word against mine," he said to Harry. "We'll be in the brig together. I can take it. I bet you won't be able to when the other bastards learn who you are."

Harry picked up the bread knife and grinned at Fischer.

"Something else you don't know about Kate," he said. "Not only is she a crack shot, but she also has connections in high places. I think it's safe to say you're screwed, Fischer."

"Where now, Harry," said Kate. "Pahiatua Police Station?"

"Perfect," he said. "We'll put him in the truck, and I'll drive there. You take your car. Do you think you can manage that?"

"I think so," she said. "Just don't drive on the wrong side of the road. I don't want you to have another accident."

21

Separation

The bar of The Hotel St. George was crowded with uniformed men, mostly US Marines who had seconded the hotel for sleeping quarters. Harry stood at the entrance looking for someone who might be Kate's father. He wouldn't be wearing a uniform, and he'd have to be in his fifties or older.

A tall man with dark wavy hair shot through with gray came towards him with his hand out, smiling. His resemblance to Kate was slight, but Harry could see her face in his. Something about his dark eyes and certainly his hair. He was a strong-looking man with broad shoulders and an air of authority.

"Major Wilhelm? Sam Hardy. Glad you could make it. We're in the Palm Lounge. Follow me."

Harry followed him into the Palm Lounge, a large ballroom with potted palms dotted about and a stage at one end. The room was empty now but looked well-used. In a corner near the entrance, a man in a dark blue uniform was seated at a large round table intended for six. He rose to greet them. A police officer. Harry felt a faint apprehension. Something was going on, and he had a feeling he wouldn't be happy about it.

"John, let me introduce you to Major Harry Wilhelm. Major Wilhelm, this is Superintendent John Foster of the Wellington Police. I'm not sure if you've spoken."

Harry shook the hand of the man who was his boss, the Superintendent of Police Captain Bates had kept mentioning. He was much less imposing than Hardy, a man of medium height with a receding hairline and light, copper-colored skin. He shook Harry's hand firmly, eyeing him up and down, seemingly not liking what he saw. What had he done to cause this obvious dislike? Did he not appreciate the near-death experiences and days without sleep?

"We haven't spoken," said the superintendent. "But I've heard about you from Captain Bates and others. We owe you a vote of thanks, Major, for helping us track down the traitors in our midst. Some of them, at least."

"Who are we missing?" asked Harry.

"The US Marine," said Foster. "His body hasn't turned up, and we're starting to suspect he may have survived his fall. And survived in good enough condition to leave the area."

Harry shrugged. Someone else could tell the superintendent what had happened to the Marine. It was above his pay grade. But wherever he was now, he wasn't coming back.

"What about the men who remain in the internment camp?" he asked. "You saw the list of names, I assume?"

"Thank you for that. You may not have heard, but the victim who got the list to us, Sean Foster, was a distant relative of mine. He came out from Ireland with a letter from his father, and I got him a spot on the police force, unfortunately for him."

"No need to feel guilty, John. He volunteered," said Hardy.

"I was disappointed to see an acquaintance of mine on the list, Wilhelm. A fellow I knew from the Feilding races. We moved him and all the men from the special compound to a more secure place. The camp was not secure enough. The rest of the internees are bound for Somes Island, and Somes is impossible to leave unless you're an Olympic swimmer. Only one person tried and lived to tell the tale. But he was captured as he came ashore."

Harry thought about the tree with the notches that had acted as a ladder and how easy it had been to leave the internment camp in Pahiatua once Kate had come to his rescue. An island in the middle of a harbor would be much more difficult.

"I'm sorry about your uncle, Jens Sorensen," he said. "I spoke with him a few days ago. I understand he was suffering from shell shock. He died bravely, however."

Hardy nodded and then glanced at Superintendent Foster.

"There's something else we want to talk about, Wilhelm. I'll cut to the chase. It's about my daughter Kate. I understand you've spent some time with her lately, that you've become close."

Closer than you realize, Harry thought, remembering the previous night when he'd awoken in the early hours to find her leaning against him.

"She was great," he said. "She's a brave woman."

"Rather headstrong," said Hardy. "I wish she'd stay on the farm with my mother and not insist on working in Wellington."

"She needs to make a life of her own, surely," said Harry. "To earn her way in the world. We're in the middle of the twentieth century. Times have changed, even without the war."

"She doesn't need to earn anything," said Hardy sharply. "She's the heiress to a considerable fortune."

Harry raised his eyebrows. "Really? She didn't mention that to me."

"Why would she? And as I'm sure you know, she's engaged to a young man I hold in high esteem."

"She did tell me about Brian," said Harry. "Isn't he missing in action in Crete?"

He saw Superintendent Foster's hand tighten on his drink.

"He's my son," he said, glaring at Harry. "He's missing, but we believe he made it to the Cretan resistance. Several men in his company did. And there's been no report of his death from the Germans. They always report the dead and the injured."

Harry felt as if he'd been punched in the gut. Why had Kate not told him that the man overseeing his assignment was Brian's father? He could see what was going on now. He'd been called in not for praise or thanks but because they wanted to warn him off. They had decided their offspring would marry each other and connect the two families. Did Brian also come from a wealthy family? Probably.

"I'm sorry about your son," he said. "You're right about the Germans. They keep excellent records, and they report everything."

"You'd know, I suppose," said Hardy. He looked at Harry, his eyes narrowing. "What with your father being a colonel in the Waffen-SS."

"I haven't had any contact with my father since I was a child," said Harry. A colonel in the SS, for fuck's sake. He should have known. His grandparents should have told him. Nimitz must know. That was why he'd been sent here, where he could cause the least trouble and also prove his loyalty. Fighting with Carlson's Raiders had not been enough for them. He'd wondered what he was doing here ever since he'd arrived. Now he knew.

"Under the circumstances," said Hardy, "I'd prefer that you

stay away from my daughter. We're grateful for all you've done, and to show there are no hard feelings, we want you to continue as a liaison between the US Marine Corps and our government. However, we've caught everyone in this area, and they'll know about you, so we're sending you elsewhere. We think there's some kind of assassination plot in the offing, and you'll be assisting us with preventing that. It involves someone from your country — America, I mean, not Germany."

Harry had nothing to say. If he refused to cooperate, they'd send him back to the Pacific war zone, and he'd never see Kate again. If he agreed with their plan, at least they'd be in the same country. Not that he didn't want to fight, but who knew what might happen when Brian came home? She'd be lonely.

"Where am I going?" he asked, wondering how far they could send him. The South Island? The Fijian Islands? Maybe even New Caledonia? "And when am I leaving?"

"North," said the superintendent. "You're to report to the Auckland Police in two days. We have a sleeper ticket waiting for you at the railway station for the overnight train. It leaves at eleven tonight. Please don't contact Kate before you leave."

* * *

"You did what?" Kate said to her father. "You sent Harry away? After he's done so much for us? Is it because Superintendent Foster wanted you to? Because of Brian?"

"Kate, I know it's been a long time since you saw Brian, but there's a good chance he'll come home eventually. He won't be happy if you've already had a child with this American, who won't hang around if you do. He's an American. He's out for what he can get."

Kate looked at her father, shocked.

"You have the wrong end of the stick, completely," she said. "I don't give a damn what Brian thinks if and when he comes home. But I do care what Harry thinks. He's the man I intend to marry, even if I have to wait for years until the war has ended and even if I have a child with him before then."

"You're so stubborn, Kate. I'm sure you felt the same way about Brian when you agreed to marry him before he left for Greece."

"I didn't agree to marry him. He made that up. We spent one night together, and I hated it. But afterward, he thought he owned me."

Sam Hardy's jaw dropped.

"You slept with Brian, Kate?"

She sighed and stared at the floor. "I didn't mean to, but he told me he didn't want to die without knowing what it was like, and I felt obliged to agree. All the women felt the same way. You must know how it was. You went through a war yourself."

She could see her father wavering.

"I know you want to join our families, but I'm not a princess who has to marry for political reasons. I thought you'd understand. Please tell his father I'm not waiting for Brian and I'm in love with Harry Wilhelm."

He sighed. "I'll tell him, but he won't believe me. He's determined that you two will marry."

"Thank you. And can you also tell me where you sent Harry?"

"I'm sorry, Kate, but I can't. Foster invoked the Official Secrets Act. All I can say is he's liaising with the police in the north of New Zealand. You'll have to find him yourself, but I'm sure you will. And I'll do what I can to help, I promise."

SEPARATION

* * *

The newsroom was quiet as usual. Kate marched between the desks of the old men, feeling as if she'd never left. Most of them looked as if they hadn't even changed positions. One or two opened their eyes and nodded a greeting.

Max was in his office, and he looked up with a grin when she dropped the keys to the Roadster on his desk.

"My, my, I hear you've been busy. Did the Roadster survive? Are you back for good? What was going on at Camp Russell? The S.I.B. called and said I was not to publish anything. But you can tell me everything, can't you?"

"Not much happened," she said airily. "A couple of murders, a kidnapping, some German spies, a bit of romance. You know, the usual stuff."

He chuckled. "You have a vivid imagination, Kate. But one of these days, you'll tell me the truth, I swear you will."

"Maybe I will," she said. "But I'm going to have to spend some time researching something first, which will involve many long-distance telephone calls. I hope you can handle the costs."

"Take all the time you need and ring whoever you want," he said. "I'm sure there's a story, and I want it."

"You'll get it, I promise," said Kate.

When the war's over, she added, under her breath.

She had something else to do before writing a story about what had happened at the camp. And that was to find Harry. And she would find him, even if it meant ringing every newspaper in the country.

THE END

Thank you for reading this first book in a new series. I intend to write three books for this series, possibly more if I have the energy! The next book, A Very Important Person, is due to be published on June 1, 2025.

And don't worry about Harry. She'll find him.

22

Author's Note

I learned that the US Marines were in New Zealand during World War Two quite recently. I had a vague idea that the American army was in my home country in the 1940s, mostly because my mother always claimed to have had "opportunities" when she was living alone with my brother during the war. My father fought in the Pacific, including a stint in the Solomon Islands, but as far as I know, she did not take advantage of those opportunities. I was born in Pahiatua in 1946 and knew nothing about the internment camp, which became a camp for refugee Polish children in 1947. Children we called Displaced Persons, or DPs, were familiar to me then.

I was researching an idea for a book set in World War Two when I came across the tragedy of the drownings in Paekākāriki on the west coast of the North Island, and I knew immediately that I had to write a book that included the event.

I was not the first person to think that the US Marine Corps in New Zealand would be a good idea for a book. In 1953, Leon Uris published *Battle Cry*, based on his own experiences in WW2, which included his time in New Zealand. He would not have known about the accident with the landing craft, however, because it was hushed up until some years after the war.

Don Adams of *Get Smart* fame also spent time in New Zealand during the war. After enlisting at fifteen, he caught Malaria on Guadalcanal and recovered in an American hospital in Lower Hutt, outside Wellington.

Printed in Great Britain
by Amazon